Other books by Merlinda Bobis

Banana Heart Summer
Available from Delta

and

Pag-uli, Pag-uwi, Homecoming (poetry)
A Novel-in-Waiting (monograph)
White Turtle/The Kissing (short fiction)
Summer Was a Fast Train Without Terminals (poetry)
Cantata of the Warrior Woman Daragang Magayon (poetry)
*Ang Lipad ay Awit sa Apat na Hangin/Flight Is Song on
Four Winds* (poetry)
Rituals (poetry)

THE SOLEMN LANTERN MAKER

THE SOLEMN
LANTERN MAKER

A NOVEL

Merlinda Bobis

delta trade paperbacks

A Delta Trade Paperback Original

Published in the United States by Delta Trade Paperbacks, an imprint of The Random House Publishing Group, a division of Random House, Inc., New York.

Delta is a registered trademark of Random House, Inc., and the colophon is a trademark of Random House, Inc.

Originally published in Australia by Pier 9, an imprint of Murdoch Books Pty Limited, Sydney, in 2008.

Library of Congress Cataloging-in-Publication Data

Bobis, Merlinda C. (Merlinda Carullo)
   The solemn lantern maker / Merlinda Bobis.
      p. cm.
   ISBN 978-0-385-34113-4 (trade pbk.)
   1. Boys—Philippines—Fiction. 2. Americans—Philippines—Fiction.
3. Philippines—Fiction. I. Title.
   PR9550.9.B58S65 2009
   823'.914—dc22

                                                                    2009009636

Printed in the United States of America

www.bantamdell.com

9 8 7 6 5 4 3 2 1

Text designed by Diane Hobbing of Snap-Haus Graphics

For the Nolands and Eugenes
of this world.
I wish you wings.

They stretched their willing wings,
and gladly sped from their bright seats above,
to tell the shepherds on the hillside at night,
the marvellous story. . . .

Not with the stammering tongue of him
that tells a story in which he has no interest;
nor even with the feigned interest of a man
that would move the passions of others,
when he feels no emotion himself;
but with joy and gladness,
such as angels only can know.

They "sang" the story out. . . .

The First Christmas Carol
Charles H. Spurgeon (1834–92)

DECEMBER 19

1

A star has five lights. Noland thinks it so it must be true. Angels live in stars, with fire in their chests. So when they breathe, the sky twinkles. Noland thinks hard what he can't say as he runs from car to car, peddling his own version of stars. Around him, the festive business rises to fever pitch — "Only six days to Christmas, ma'am, sir, so you're getting these cheap. You can't miss out, only six days."

How dare anyone miss out? At this intersection of the highway, star lanterns made of translucent *capiz* shells outshine each other, desperate to be sold. Red, green, gold, and pearly white blink and whirl with electric lights, like stained glass on speed. The shoppers' faces catch the glow. So does Noland's. It is a solemn face, like those of plaster saints who endure years of silent watching.

"Hoy, you're blocking my customers!" a stall owner scolds the boy, who steadies his wooden cart of lanterns. His are made of Japanese paper, small stars with two frilly tails instead of lights. "Are you serious?" one shopper asks, looking incredulously from the boy's simple wares to the giant creation she bought for six thousand pesos. Heaven should be grand, boy, and bringing it down to earth is costly business. "Hoy, over here!" a man calls out from an old Mitsubishi. Finally, a customer. "How much?" he asks, while peeling a pork bun.

Noland raises five fingers thrice to indicate fifteen pesos.

Intent on his dinner, the man does not see the price. "How much?" he asks again. Noland raises his palm close to the man's face, repeating the gesture.

The man pauses, stares —

Palm as small as a star, star as small as a country.

Now where did that come from? He's becoming a poet.

Steam rises from the bun. Noland imagines the pork stew and the salted egg inside. He hands the man a red star, eyes on the first bite. Is the yolk bigger than the white? The man pays with a fifty-peso bill. Noland shakes his head and shows an empty palm. No change, sorry sir. Perhaps two more stars? He offers a green one this time and another red.

"No, keep the change." He waves the boy away and hangs the star on his window, just above the wheel. Then as an afterthought, "You mute, kid?"

The ten-year-old nods.

The man sighs, taking in the face that is too gaunt, too serious for a child.

My country's children small as hope.

2

"Of course yours are the real thing, because you make them in the old style," his friend Elvis assures him. "Small stars but specially homemade by the master star maker, so gimme five!" Then the customary palm-slapping before turning his baseball cap at a jaunty angle and running toward the traffic.

Noland wonders about his friend's exceptional gift. He's chatting up a Pajero now. Earlier it was a Mercedes. They met only a month ago but Elvis has quickly made himself indispensable as Noland's *"parol* assistant," churning out most of the sales. His uncle Bobby Cool, with his Walkman, cell phone, and gold crucifix, has become their *"parol* godfather."

Parol is the traditional star lantern. Not for Noland, though. You call a star a star, or not at all. But of course, he can't say. Nor can he say that Bobby's donation of five hundred pesos toward his business is too generous. What if he can't sell enough lanterns to pay him back? But uncle and nephew assured him that business would grow if they worked together like family. Noland grew warm inside when he heard it. *Like family.* Like Christmas gift-wrapped in kind voices. They grew softer when his benefactors realized he couldn't speak. "You don't say because you're busy thinking," Elvis diagnosed his condition. "So gimme five!" Their friendship was sealed.

"Buy ah-one, ah-two, ah-homemade-star, ah-three, ah-four, ah-homemade-star." Elvis waves six lanterns at a time to the passing cars, stabbing the air like a rapper revved up by attitude. "Hey, watch me, dude!"

Business has grown more desperate. It's eight in the evening and traffic has been stalled for half an hour. The flower girl pesters every car on the strip again, hoping to sell another jasmine strand for the Child Jesus on the dashboard or the altar at home, or simply to perfume the growing impatience and boredom. Drivers are forced to light up, courtesy of the cigarette man plying his wares with a Christmas trumpet. The duck-egg and the quail-egg vendors are fighting for territory, and an old man is selling more than his hand-mops. He's mopping the car windows himself as street kids run up and down the traffic, begging and singing "Jingle Bells." One window opens and the kids rush to the car, but the oldest girl with a baby gets there first. The driver scolds her for dragging the baby along, then gives her a ten-peso bill. She whines about her sick sister and holds out the baby's palm for more. The driver curses, and the window is shut.

The boys sell as many stars as the "official" lantern

vendors. Parked beside the stalls, the cart is *their stall* and they can run from car to car with their smaller wares. Noland feels his pockets grow. Elvis's "gimme fives" multiply. He does the hand-slapping ritual with Noland after each sale, for next-time luck. While Bobby stands by, he chats up a Kombi van. The tinted window half rolls down and the driver buys all the lanterns in his hand.

Noland marvels at his friend's ability. Their cart might be empty yet before tonight is over. Bobby Cool doesn't think this marvelous, just normal. He trusts his twelve-year-old protégé, who now turns his cap at all angles, reporting on his transactions. Bobby approves and gives the boy a shove—back to work. Then he gets on the phone and slinks away.

3

Nerves are even more frayed. The traffic just won't move. Is there an accident somewhere? Cell phones ring and get rung. Drivers grow quarrelsome. Lantern bargainers get overwrought and the street kids' "Jingle Bells" sounds more driven, a militant Christmas wish for more grace, more grace from your pockets. Those who protest by turning up the Christmas carols on their stereos are admonished by blaring horns. Hoy, some peace, please, it's bad enough as it is!

"Hey, over here!" It takes a while for the foreign voice to be heard. It's from a taxi, in front of the man with the pork bun.

Noland stares.

"Yes, you please, over here," the voice calls out.

It's a woman with golden hair, with a very white face, with a hand stretched out toward him. The most beautiful creature. An angel!

But Elvis gets there first, cap quickly adjusted to a jauntier angle. "Hey, beautiful lady, wanna buy?" He waves at the cart and the stalls of lanterns as if he's the godfather of all the shining stars. "They *parol* all for lady—"

"*Pa-rol?*" She points to the swirl of lights.

"Yes, ma'am, but my *parol* more bee-yoo-ti-ful like lady," Elvis declaims, offering his own stars, bunches in both hands. He sashays before the stranger so she can inspect the goods.

Noland is stunned by his friend's boldness. Elvis even drapes himself on the taxi door and the angel laughs nervously. "You love New York?" she asks.

Elvis is perplexed. "New York? Me no go there, ma'am."

"Your cap." She points. "It says, 'I love New York.'"

"Oh yes, Elvis love New York," he confirms, preening.

"Your name's Elvis?" The angel laughs a little more heartily, then continues, "So, Elvis, what are they made of?" She is after the lit stars and this peeves the boy, but he's quick to respond. "Shell, *capiz* shell—but my *parol* more cute, see?" He waves the paper stars under her nose, but she keeps looking beyond them, thinking shining flowers more than stars. She tests the words in her head, imagines them blooming. *Pa-rol. Ca-piz.*

"They shine so—so—" She sighs.

Noland hangs onto this exhalation of awe, to the look that goes with it. She glows, she glows. But Elvis is intent on only one thing. He opens the taxi door with a mock bow. "Okay, beautiful lady want big star, Elvis take beautiful lady to big star, no problem—but she buy small star from Elvis, okay?"

Noland peers behind the older boy, holding his breath. She's about to alight. Under the headlights of the pork bun man's car, her hair swirls like a halo!

But she pulls back her feet, changing her mind.

"Is okay, Elvis stop traffic for beautiful lady, is okay," and he bows deeper with a little flourish of his cap.

"It's okay?" the white woman asks her driver who quickly responds, "No problem—traffic not moving, traffic dead." He chuckles, liking his joke.

The angel walks a few paces from her taxi. She's asking something, but Noland can't hear any more. Behind them, a Pizza Hut motorcycle revs close to the pork bun man, then suddenly three shots break the traffic drone and the man slumps over the wheel, making his newly bought star dance and Pizza Hut revs past, hitting the angel who collapses. She's shot too she's shot and Noland is rushing to her rushing with his cart of lanterns picking her up where did he get his strength lifting her into the cart with Elvis pushing her from the screaming the shocked "Jingle Bells" the silenced cars the halted buying and selling and the man bleeding at the wheel wondering why the star is growing smaller dimmer and where does this thought come from?

Palm as small as a star, star as small as a country. How small.

4

"She's shot, Noland—*putang 'na,* what're you doing? She's shot, you hear me? Ay, ay, all this blood, look, shit man, you can't take her home. You're crazy, you'll— we'll get into trouble. Shit-shit-shit!"

I'm being cursed, I'm cursed. The American picks up only one English word fading with the stars, no, the shining flowers, but all dark now, all dark. . . .

"What if she dies?"

Noland maneuvers the cart behind a stall from where the vendor has bolted, screaming, "Ay, sniper, sniper!" Here the boy quickly covers the cart with a plastic sheet that he uses for rain. She's hidden now, folded like a doll in a cart being pushed toward the slums along the railway track. Behind them, police sirens wail. He breaks into a sprint, the wail chasing him. It pierces his ears, spills inside his skull.

"Hoy, you crying, Noland—for a stranger?"

Grief follows the sharp contour of a cheek, a faint trembling there, but the overlarge eyes are alert, picking out bumps and dips on the ground. It's a face that's all planes and angles, and so is the body that pushes away from the sirens. What if she dies, what if she dies?

"You're crazy, Noland." Elvis puffs beside him, his cap and the world gone awry. The railway track has stretched longer, mocking their feet, too small, too clumsy for flight. The huts are racing too, blurring beside them like the yelled-out censure from a window, "Hoy, slow down, you crazies!"

Two red shirts are hurtling through, one shabby, the other less so. The squealing cart sets the teeth on edge. It has saved hundreds of bottles, cartons, plastic, everything that a city can shed, but with no heroic ambition. The patchwork of wood and motorcycle wheels knows its place, pushed around by the boy since he was eight to public dumps or the backstreet bins of restaurants. But not at Christmas, when he can sleep without the scent of discarded lives on his skin. In this season, he rises from the dump, deals in stars. Almost of the sky.

But the older boy has no illusions. "Shit, man, you'll get us into shit-shit-shit and we'll both be dead-ball." His mouth is dry, his ranting incoherent.

"Shut up, baby's trying to sleep!" Another censure nearby.

Noland's grip on the cart tightens. It rattles and squeaks louder, protesting over its burden. Anytime it might give, like him. His hands are sticky with blood; so are his clothes. His pace picks up—almost there, almost there.

What if the feet forget their use, lift from the ground and get carried away by a whim or a wish? The cart will just have to put up with it.

"Okay, I'm with you, if that's what you wish in that crazy-crazy head."

Suddenly a firecracker goes off and the cart squeals to a halt.

5

It's a box, the poorest in the slums. It's scraps of corrugated iron, wood, cardboard, and plastic, and a hole for a door, set apart from the rest of the huts, because here's where all the sewage flows. The creek of fetid water is everyone's toilet, everyone's dump.

Outside children are setting off firecrackers. The oldest one, Mikmik, calls out, "Why so early? Sold all your dwarf stars—ha-ha-ha!"

"Shuddup!" Elvis growls as Noland pushes the cart to the back of the hut. Here washing lines run to a wire fence separating the slums from the highway, where the chaos from the shooting has quickly spilled over.

"So what do we do?" Elvis whispers through gritted teeth. There's no back door and they can't use the front with all those nosy children around. Noland begins to pull a piece of corrugated iron from the wall to make a door.

Elvis can't believe his eyes. "You're really way out."

The hut looks as if it's about to collapse. Inside a woman calls out, "Who's there? That you, son?"

"Ah, you'll catch it this time," Elvis says.

The corrugated iron won't come off. Noland motions for Elvis to shut up and wait. He runs to the front and enters the hut. Elvis hears the mother scolding, then after a pause she yells at the children outside to go away because she's sick and needs to rest. The children protest and call her a witch but soon amble away, still setting off firecrackers.

Noland rushes back to the cart. They wait for the place to clear and soon haul the white woman into the hut, half wrapped in the plastic.

Nena swallows a scream—so much blood! "*Dios ko,* my God, what did you do to that—that—?"

"*Putang 'na,* it wasn't us!"

"Don't you swear at me, Elvis, you good-for-nothing—"

"Sorry-sorry, she was shot, Aling Nena, by Pizza Hut, Aling Nena—is she dead?" Elvis steps back. Nena has never liked him.

"Take that away." Her voice rises. "Ay, ay, you good-for-nothing kids, always picking up trouble, hoy, what trouble did you get my son into? Take that away, I want no police here, no uniforms, take that away!"

The son's hand on his mother's mouth is gentle but firm. His eyes plead, gurgling sounds rise from his throat. Mother and son are locked in a silent argument, gaunt faces mirroring each other. Her chest feels like it will burst as she watches her son organize the "Amerkana" like an efficient somnambulist. First unroll the mat on the floor, lift her onto it with Elvis's help, get a towel, wipe off the blood—Nena stops him and takes the towel from his hands. For the first time, she looks closely at the white woman. Maybe thirties. Very blond hair stained with blood, ugly bruise on the left temple, spreading beyond the hairline perhaps to the back of the head. Looks like a very bad fall, which she probably tried to break with her arms, also bruised and bloodied. But the pink top is not as messy as the white slacks. The blood is mostly around the lower torso, between and down the legs.

Nena picks out bits of star clinging to the still body.

"You think she's dead?" Elvis whispers.

She feels for a pulse, then gently pushes at the woman's belly. The woman groans.

"She's alive, Noland, she's alive!" Elvis returns to the fold, taking off his cap respectfully. "We saved her!"

Noland presses his heart with his fists. The beating must be knocked back, silenced for this occasion. Of course, she's only sleeping.

Neither of the boys catches the strange look on Nena's face. She lets out a big breath before telling them to change out of those bloodied things. "*Sige*, fetch me

some water, both of you, quick—no, she was *not* shot."
She crawls to a box for some rags and maybe clothes for
the stranger, her legs dragging behind. Times like this,
they hurt, how they hurt.

6

It's a magical house. Elvis couldn't believe his eyes when
he first came to visit. Inside, wood, cardboard, and corrugated iron are papered with pictures of angels and
stars from magazines and billboards. Poor walls
patched up into some kind of heaven, and up in the roof,
or the bits and pieces that try to be a roof, Noland's star
lanterns hanging from rows and rows of strings, like
festive laundry. Then a bamboo Christmas tree, also
Noland's handiwork, painted white for snow and hung
with thumb-sized stars. The main bamboo pole has a little window carved midway along its hollow trunk.
Here, tucked at the center of the tree, is a milk can with
holes. Inside the can, a lit candle, its light streaming
through. It is the heart of the tree, a flickering innova-
tion of a heart.

It is this lit heart that the American catches through
half-closed lids. Or did she just dream it? Like the ten-
der hand wiping her aching belly, making her less sad
about something that she's now forgetting. Everything
is slipping away. Even her landing at Ninoy Aquino

International Airport only a few hours ago and how she rang home to her husband—how stupid of her.

"I'm fine—I just landed—I'm fine, on holiday of course—and—and don't worry, I'm fine...*we're* fine." Harder to speak to an answering machine when you're crying, but even this has gone now, even how she stood for a long time before a star flashing like a multicolored alarm warning her not to ring again. Then at Customs, a two-man band was conjuring Rudolph and his sleigh—everything's slipping away like the blood washed off by a stranger's hand finding even her secret parts. Who is to say what we can hide and reveal to others and to ourselves, when even the body wants to forget?

"You've no right to come to us like this," Nena mutters to herself as she rinses the bloodied rag in the pail. "You've no right to make us remember."

Does the American hear? The boy who saved her is still telling himself that she's only sleeping. He's outside now, listening to his friend's false bravado, watching him turn his cap at all possible angles.

"She could've died, you know, if not for us—you think she has lots of money?" Elvis rummages in his pocket for a cigarette. "White people have lots of money—ah, Noland, you just don't know." He lights up and takes in a lungful like a pro, then blows at his friend's face. "Relax, we saved the Amerkana. Isn't that great?" He giggles nervously. "I think she's Amerkana—trust me, I know their talk—I know Americans, Australians, Germans, Japanese, yeah man, I know many-many in-

ternational but America's the best, so cool, like this cigarette — see, it's super cool, like New York, man, I love
New York." He giggles even more, slapping his thigh,
then turning with the usual gesture. "So gimme five!"

Noland doesn't welcome the open palm, lest he betray how wet his hands are. He sits on them, eyes dart-
ing up and down the railway track at the neighbors
now trooping to the intersection. They've heard of the
shooting and the pile-up that followed as everyone
tried to flee the scene. The festive spirit is edgy, shrill.
Something *is* happening, really happening! There's
Helen and her husband Mario, abandoning their video
hut of pirated films and taking their patrons with
them, all primed for the live action over at the intersection. There's the wire-man Mang Pedring, who has
lit those star lanterns, imagining a disaster of smashed
merchandise. There's the nightly gin party from
Mang Gusting's store, broken up by a shot of something even more fiery — just who died, bro? There are
the karaoke women, washerwomen by day, led by Lisa-
oh-oh!, who's not quite sure whether she's sighing "oh-
oh" or saying yes "*o-o*" to fate and its machinations, like
this terrible, terrible crime. There's Manang Betya finishing the rosary, her cries for heavenly intercession
growing more desperate. And there are the children
trailing behind, their Christmas trumpets and firecrackers heralding something louder around the corner. Even the littlest ones are out, suckled on their
mothers' breasts, eavesdropping on the rise and fall of

stories: the conjectures, the gossip, the tales taller than any action film.

"Hoy, Noland, I better join them now." Elvis makes a move to go. "Must get back to work, yeah, man," he adds, winking, and Noland can't say that work's over for the night, that he has to clean up the cart and throw out the bloodied stars, that he can't come with him now. His hands are wet, his pants are even wetter, but in the dark his friend can't see; nor can he know.

7

The angels are watching over a boy, a mother, and a stranger. The cherub on the ceiling is smiling through rain stains. It's from a soap ad, not quite as heavenly as the Christmas angel that lost its trumpet. This cut-out from a billboard covers a gap in the door, between wood and corrugated iron. Above the kerosene stove is a sooty Saint Michael, the trademark of Ginebra San Miguel, a cheap gin, with his sword raised to slay the devil under his feet. In another corner is Saint Raphael, the archangel with the fish, looming from a 1996 calendar as if to say, "Here, fish for supper." His wings have peeled with age but a new pair has been drawn over in pencil.

These were homeless angels once. The boy found

them in the public dump. He was eight and they were living in another slum when he found his first angel. He had scurried up a moving garbage truck along with ten other kids and the driver was yelling, "You want to kill yourselves?" but they were all stuck into it, scavenging, checking out, and choosing. Then he saw her being tossed back and forth by two giggling boys. She was a Christmas angel, he could tell from the trumpet and the still joyful face despite the dirt. She was as tall as the boys, a billboard from last Christmas. She's my girlfriend, no she's mine, she loves me, no, me, me! The boys played their little game until the truck pulled to a halt and they got back to work, tossing her aside. She landed in the mud, still blowing her trumpet, which quickly slipped into a puddle. Noland had to jump off the truck before the puddle claimed her too.

She was wet. The trumpet broke off entirely when he lifted her into the cart. It had rained last night and it was drizzling again, so he took her under "the church," as he calls it in his head. The large domed structure with its Roman columns looks curiously out of place in the dumping ground, which used to be a cemetery. Perhaps it was once a mausoleum. Beside it, some niches still stand. He used to play here often, alone, hide-and-seek with the silent dead. The other children didn't like the mute boy in their games.

Under his church, he cleaned her up, then brought

her home. He thought she looked perfect at the door, standing just so, even without the trumpet. He cut out stars from an old magazine and pasted them around her. Later, he found the other angels. When they moved to the railway tracks, he refused to leave them behind. The new home was perfect, more so at Christmas when the lantern stalls along the highway lit up like heaven. He cut out more stars, pasted them around the hut. Then he dared to be extravagant.

One Christmas, he bought some Japanese paper and bamboo from money earned selling his scavenged bottles. He made his first lantern, a tiny star. By a stroke of luck, he sold it to someone who had just bought a shell lantern. He happened to be standing with his star beside one of the stalls. The nice lady thought his creation "cute" and rare these days when lanterns were made of either plastic or shell. *"Parolito*—little lantern," she said, pinching his cheek. He couldn't name his price, but she gave him fifteen pesos. He was stunned. His mother wept and thanked his angels, not for the money but for the return of her boy. He was coming alive. He stopped whimpering into space, stopped wetting his pants. He made more stars. In this joy, all sorrow could only be irrelevant.

But not tonight, when the hut is waking up to old stories. There's no room for them here, no room! The angels understand; they keep to the shadows. Sometimes the flickering heart of the Christmas tree catches their intent, though less heavenly this time. They're eavesdropping, maybe on the boy's thoughts or the stranger's dreams, or the mother's anxiety. It's in her bones, gnawing at the marrow of her legs. Little mice. The angels hear them.

"Why did you bring that woman here? What's got into you? Why did you ever get friendly with that Elvis?"

The boy has grown up with his mother's anxious querying, her way of conversation, as if it could force him to answer, scold him to speak.

"Hoy, can you hear me? Elvis is big-big trouble, the devil himself." She is tiny, like a girl, but there's nothing girlish about the bony limbs, the gray hair. She keeps rubbing her legs under the long housedress, from calves to thighs. She can hide them from the eyes, but this pain, this pain — "Why don't you listen to me? I know what's good for you. Hoy, are you listening?"

He is listening to the white woman's breathing.

"Tomorrow she must go. When she wakes up, she's out — I'll have no police here, no uniforms. You hear me?" She sits still, listening to the police sirens going off again, then scrapes the last mouthful of rice from her plate on the floor. Her hand shakes as she brings it to her mouth. "And eat your dinner! You think we can afford to waste food like this?"

Her son waits for each rise and fall of the stranger's chest. Nena watches him, wants to drag him back — eat your dinner! She shifts her useless legs. Times like this, they remind her that they're still here, useful for remembering... times like this.

He squats at his guest's feet, watching over her long after his mother blows out the candle in the Christmas tree. This isn't the only light in the hut. Sometimes the television works. He found it too, in the dump, when he went early before the other scavengers arrived. Mario, who runs the video hut across the tracks, fixed it. It's dented all over and the black-and-white picture often disappears; the boy pounds it with his fist to make it come on again. When it's on, his mother does not scold and all's well with the world. Of course they only watch it when they can pay Mang Pedring, who's in charge of the street's illegal wirings. The wire-man can fix up any electrical connection secretly and disconnect it just as discreetly, and promptly if you don't pay.

"Leave her alone, son, and come to bed. Tomorrow she'll go." The mother has spread some cardboard on the floor, an arm's length from their only mat, where the white woman sleeps. If she reaches out, she'll touch her face. Is it still wet? She cried the whole time Nena was washing her. Maybe she wanted her eyes washed too, though she never opened them.

"Noland..." the mother calls out. She's afraid he will sit forever with the stranger in this familiar pose, watching in the dark—no, we can't go back there. Ay, why did *you* come? There's no room for you here.

There is no room for another time. The hut is too

small even for the present. Life must be squeezed to pocket size, breath must be kept spare, so there's enough left for the next day, so the walls hold up. Be frugal where life is fragile. Tears are an imposition here.

8

Hands open in supplication or fold close to the chest in prayer, but sometimes it's closer to play. Tap each other's hands and clap:

Star-light, star-bright
Make-a-wish-a-wish-tonight.

But tonight there's no star-light, star-bright over the slums. The sky is too murky and the city lights too bright. Back on the farm, they watched each star come out, rising from the hill just above the fields of rice that her husband planted. "Those are angels," she told her son, "watching over the rice so it can turn to gold, watching over the land so it can be safe." Before sleeping, they invoked heaven with the little play of hands. These days she only scolds: "I want you safe." This is prayer too, just as wishful, just as anxious.

"Star-light, star-bright..." It plays in Noland's head. He has his own worry, his own wish. How can his mother dress an angel in rags?

Outside the midnight train is passing at top speed. Briefly earth and heaven conspire for the eyes. The ramshackle huts and their tinseled trees, the parallel highway with shining stars at each lamppost, the lantern stalls, the zipping cars, the last street vendors and beggars, all collect in a blur for the passengers who are nodding off to sleep. The train rocks them, rocks all the dreams it carries and passes, rocks them into one, and the earth shudders at the weight of this suddenly singular life.

Noland closes his eyes, paces his breath with his guest's, his face rapt, caught in the attitude of intense listening. Then he hears it. "That's good, that's good," says the rise and fall in the American's chest. He is relieved. What he can't say, he thinks hard. What he thinks hard, he tells in comic strips: stars and angels framed in hundreds of little story boxes strung together since he found his first angel, four years after he lost his speech. His comic strips are unusual, each story frame flowing into the next with no gaps in between, except the page breaks. It's really only *one* story, like the angels and stars that he's brought into the hut or drawn in his notebook. His mother knows about it but pretends she doesn't. He hides the notebook, hides the stories that he's conjured, like this one. He does not need a light to draw this quick tale, which he does now in three boxes coming to life in black ballpoint.

Four stars in the sky.

Angel falling from the fourth star.
Angel on the pavement and three stars in the sky.
It is the cosmic reduced to the simplest terms.

9

Hush, I know a story you don't know. The conspiracy of silence leaves the angels breathless in their watching. They see the boy hide the notebook again and crawl back to his guest. But she's too long for this mat, this blanket, her feet stick out! It worries him. Should he find something else to cover her feet? But it will be only some old towel or rag, even more shameful than these worn bedclothes, which never bothered him before.

A quick sensation in his gut perplexes the boy. He does not know that it is shame, this squirming inside for the first time, because he cannot offer more. He turns slightly toward the corner where the television sits, an unconscious move for reassurance toward his priceless possession. It makes him feel sort of rich. All rich people have televisions—look, we have a TV too!

The boy shrugs, crawls to where his mother is sleeping and lies down. He can't make the mat or the blanket grow longer, can he? He can't complete the act of kindness yet. Later, in his dream, he will save her but not her feet, and what a shame. It's a pity tonight he does not trust the angels in the hut. But when they breathe, do they not kindle the fires in their chests? And light up the hut, as they light up the night? He put them here in the first place, did he not? Still undeniably of heaven and regal despite the soot and stain, the missing trumpet, the repaired wings. But perhaps tonight is too dark for faith. "Real angels" are meant to be all clean and bright, complete and white.

The white woman tosses and turns, not about her naked feet but her empty womb.

In the early hours of the morning, the mother wakes. The cardboard is wet, her son is wet. He does not stir when she changes his pants. She bites her lip the whole time. The hut is too small; there is no room to weep.

DECEMBER 20

DECEMBER

10

Keep it shut. Keep it dark. Keep it perpetually night. From the time the unknown American is taken in by Noland, it seems as if day will never be allowed in the hut. His mother insists on total secrecy, lest the police, the uniforms, come. She feels it in her bones, this old panic, as if her limbs were being pulled apart and anytime they'd snap. She insists the stranger must leave when she wakes up.

When she wakes up. In his head Noland conjures scenes of wonder, of wondrous blessings, for she's an angel, isn't she? But first she must eat. He checks the two pieces of *pan de sal*—oh, to have some proper meat for a sandwich. What do angels eat? He frowns at the glass of water beside the bread. Some Milo soon, yes, Milo's good. He knows this drink so well from the TV ad: Go-go-go Milo! He tries to tidy up, but there's not much to tidy. The hut is only a little longer than the sleeping guest and as wide as two of her arm spans maybe, and certainly much below her height.

Noland worries about the piles of boxes, the lantern papers strewn around, the stove, the television, and even the Christmas tree sitting on it. They all seem to take up so much space now. How will she fit, when she wakes up? Will she see that half of the floor is dirt? The wooden planks once rescued from a demolished stadium haven't made enough floor. He retrieves some of his hanging stars to cover the floorless part, a bit of heaven to conceal the earth, but how he wishes they had a light-bulb. A TV but no proper light—but a TV anyway, he reminds himself, giving the box a good wipe.

It is six in the morning. The only lights in the hut are pinpoints from the cracks and an opaque glow behind the patches of plastic and paper. On the roof, a spot on the cherub's brow, a little sun the size of a coin, and where the corrugated iron door joins with the wood, a line of light cutting the pasted angel in half, then the few pinpoints streaming in, exposing a detail here and there. A corner of the stove, a clump of paper stars above, and even the American's face almost catching light, Noland hopes, if he moves her just a bit. She must be *with* the light—but, he relents, she must rest. Anyway when she wakes, when she finally moves, it will be real morning. He draws little scenes in his head, all good tidings, all bright.

Outside the train passes, the hut trembles.

He proceeds to make more lanterns, smoothing out the Japanese paper with the tenderness of a craftsman. He will sell more stars tonight, he must. He checks on his guest again, inspired with plans that make him smile to himself. The watching angels know the smile, rare for this boy. If only he could see himself, that he looks like them, almost, when his lips break their solemn repose.

"Noland, Noland!" It's Elvis banging at the door, making him jump. Quickly he sneaks his friend in, gesticulating that he must not, *must not ever,* tell anyone about their guest, or else—but Elvis calms the flailing hands with a McDonald's bag handed over with a swagger, see what I brought, then quickly takes out a burger himself, oh, I haven't had breakfast myself, while telling stories about the crime scene last night when he returned to it and how Bobby Cool was so angry they both disappeared, but he took care of everything and of course he won't tell Bobby about the white woman—so, is she awake?

No, she's not! Elvis overacts his disappointment, shaking his head dismally. "What do we do with her, Noland? You think she has plenty of money?"

But Noland is busy peeking into the bag. He finds the other burger, which he lays beside the two bread buns, for when she wakes. He's pleased with his friend. He gives him a pat on the head.

"No!" Elvis protests. "I told you, never touch me there—I'm no dog." He puts on his cap, turning it around so the large visor flaps like a wing from his temple. "There, how do I look? Like someone from New York, I bet—ha-ha-ha!" In between bites of the burger, he surveys the sleeping woman. "Not bad, she's quite a looker."

She's very beautiful, Noland protests in his head.

"But too pale, too thin, don't you think? And small—" He sniggers, cupping his chest with a hand.

Noland slaps the vulgar hand but Elvis just chuckles. He's used to his friend's prudishness—my God, he's a saint!

"And what's the Amerkana's name?"

Noland shakes his head, gesturing that she has been sleeping the whole time.

"Ah, then we should wake her, ask what's her name and how much she'll pay us—"

Noland pushes him away, making snarling noises in his throat.

"We deserve some reward—we saved her life!"

Noland points to the door, driving his friend out. How could you, how could you?

"Great to get a rise out of you sometimes. At least I know you're real, not that saintly poker face that drives me nuts, drives our customers away. You gotta have spirit, attitude, man, just watch me and learn. Hoy, *Santo Santito*!"—"Saint Little Saint," how Elvis mocks him sometimes. "You gotta be real, I mean flesh and blood, man, even if you can't speak—see, face speaks, face laughs, face frowns—" and he carries on, making faces at his friend, who has burrowed himself into his lantern making. Elvis takes the hint. The one-way conversation is over, so he turns on the television before Noland can stop him. "I hope you paid Mang Pedring, or else there'll be no—" But, yes, there is power and on screen is a news update about last night's shooting of Germinio de Vera, a journalist famous for his daring exposés on corruption and extra-judicial killings. The road reporter, Eugene Costa, details the scene at the intersection. The camera pans across the blinking lanterns, the dead man's car and several others in a collision after the panic. Police and medics are still rushing around. This was an hour after the shooting. The reporter confirms that there was no other fatality.

Eugene is a rookie journalist, very young and earnest. He wears a wide-eyed look, as if he's forever startled by life. "There's speculation that this is a payback shooting—but from a Pizza Hut man?"

The boys hold their breaths.

The reporter raves about the mystery of the Pizza Hut man, his intense look giving the story more weight, more urgency.

Elvis edges close to the television as if he's suddenly grown nearsighted, but Noland retreats, still clutching the red Japanese paper. It bleeds in his wet hands.

11

There are stray dogs everywhere. One sniffs Elvis's half-eaten burger. He swears at the diseased mongrel, but it only wags its tail more heartily. It's so mangy, its real color is barely recognizable.

"*Putang 'na*, get off me!" Elvis kicks the dog.

"It's only a dog, kid, a hungry dog," Mario of the video hut calls out from across the tracks.

"I'm hungry too," the boy retorts.

"What has it ever done to you?"

"Ruining my breakfast, can't you see?"

"You're not from here, I can tell." The man comes between the boy and the dog and gives him a little shove, but Elvis holds his ground.

"Hoy, it's too early to fight over a dog." It's Mario's wife, Helen. "Get back here and sort these videos."

Mario dutifully heeds the call after shaking a fist at the boy and lighting his first cigarette of the day.

Elvis makes faces. "Under the *saya*—under the skirt," he mouths at this man who won't say "no" to his wife but takes on a kid. Then he yells, "I'm not from here but I work around here and I have every right to eat my breakfast in peace!"

Helen comes out, looking bored and tired. "Aw, go home, kid," she says, balancing a huge basin of laundry on her head and picking up another pailful. "Go home and take that attitude with you. We're busy."

Elvis is going anyway, to wherever is chosen as

"home" by his self-appointed uncle, Bobby Cool. Somewhere classy, unlike this lot, hah! He snorts at the
cheek-by-jowl homes in various stages of poverty—the
shacks without walls, the patched-up huts, the few
houses with the luxury of some concrete, all decked
with cheap tinsel or lanterns and all waking up to work.

Helen walks on, careful not to step on the dog nib-
bling at its sores. Lisa, last night's karaoke queen, follows close behind, struggling with a mountain of
laundry. Manang Betya accosts them. She has switched
her rosary for a notebook to collect punters for *jueteng*,
an illegal gambling racket. Helen "rumbles" numbers to
bet on—she saw them flash on TV in her dream last
night, believe me. Dreamt numbers are lucky, but to
rumble or to bet on them in a new combination nails the
luck. Lisa advises caution against "the bloody numbers"
possibly inspired by *that* shooting, oh-oh! The women
are hushed for a while. Manang Betya crosses herself as
they walk to the water pump, passing by the hut of the
parol kambal, the lantern twins shaping shells into star
after star while arguing about what they saw last night,
what really happened. Farther on Mang Pedring, the
wire-man, is also arguing with Mang Gusting and his serious hangover from last night's party with the karaoke
women. "Your store will lose power if you don't pay up,
now!" Mang Pedring waves his pliers with a threatening
flourish. The store owner begs for a reprieve till after
Christmas because he's so broke, because this whole
track buys on credit and never pays, because his wife in

Hong Kong hasn't sent any money yet, not even a Christmas card, so please, some understanding. His daughter Mikmik yells her support, cursing the wire-man. Nearby the sweet-soy vendor adjudicates: "Ay, *Dios ko*, he's got no Christmas spirit, none at all!"

"Christmas spirit?" someone retorts from a window. It's a mother suckling her baby, who's whining because the milk won't flow—got scared too by last night's go-ings on. "What Christmas spirit? After that shooting at our doorstep?"

The men sober up and negotiate. It's almost peaceful again, until something explodes and everyone jumps.

Mikmik giggles, waving the smoking remains of a firecracker.

12

A terrified Nena won't listen to the talk about the shoot-ing. The other washerwomen and those waiting to fetch water or do their morning ablutions can't talk about anything else.

"You know, the police asked me questions last night, with the other lantern vendors—what do we have to do with *it* anyway?"

"I hope you didn't say anything stupid."

"Heaven forbid—we don't want any trouble."

"It was so bloody, my neighbor said."

"A Pizza Hut motorcycle, they said—just zipped past and bang-bang!"

"*Dios ko, Dios ko,* what will happen to us now?"

Nena shuts out the conversation with the squeaky pump, pushing the heavy wooden handle down to the hilt so the noise is louder, more abrasive. Some protest—they can't hear themselves because of this woman who's half crouching and half riding the pump when she's not crawling around. Her housedress lifts as she pumps, revealing what look like smashed knees and ugly scars up to her thighs. She's as soaked as her laundry, which she's trying to rush. She keeps scanning the crowd for a sign of her son and his cart; she wants to go home.

More news fires her distress when Lisa and Helen arrive. Lisa is attempting to explain in her usual flustered manner that Mrs. Sy has just hired her to do the laundry next week. "Oh-oh sorry, Nena, but that's life, she asked me—but she said you can still do the blankets tomorrow."

"What, you hijacked my customer?" Nena screams, pumping the water with greater ferocity. They've never seen her like this before. Helen tries to calm her but Nena's nerves are completely undone. She's hurling insults at Lisa and her string of "oh-ohs."

"Don't pretend you're sorry, you hypocrite!"

The water pumps on. It overflows from Nena's basin, splashes around, getting everyone wet. Some of the women edge away—ay, what rage. The line for water is in united uproar: "Get off that pump, it's our turn!" Ever the peacemaker, Helen blabbers that she's cooking chicken soup for lunch because her husband won a cockfight and brought home the enemy rooster, plus a new cell phone which was thrown in by the loser as, well, part of the bet—would Nena like some soup? Nena answers with a curt "No, thank you," wondering how Helen kept the sly maneuvering from her, but just like Lisa to hatch something like this.

Helen is deeply offended. She huffs and puffs through her laundry, beating-wringing the clothes with a passion to match Nena's. It takes a while for gossip to resume, with some nervous giggles at first but soon the storytelling aplomb absorbs even the dog now curled within eavesdropping distance. Invention grows bizarrely delightful, this weaving of tale after tall tale around the Pizza Hut man who must have been cheated by his customer, meaning the victim of course, who probably failed to pay for a pizza delivery not once but several times, you never know what people are capable of, but what if the Pizza Hut man was aiming for the lantern sellers or the blinking lanterns themselves, the lights make you dizzy-crazy sometimes, the shooting happened around the stalls remember, or what if he was after one of our men who crossed him in a drinking spree, maybe over some girl who mocked his pizzas, you never know, but who could he be, who could do such a thing so close to Christmas, ay JesusMaryandJoseph, preserve us all!

There is something comforting about gossip. It's loose, glib, and companionably intimate. It out-absurds life, rendering it less menacing. It makes us almost brave, daring to imagine the worst and our capacity to outdo it. It is our collective punt against misfortune. How comforting for tongues to wag as one.

Not if one knows the real story, though. Cut off from the herd that doesn't know any better, one is hopelessly unanchored while chained to the truth. Nena rinses the clothes from Mrs. Sy. She will come to this water pump tomorrow for the last time, and from then on a regular income lost. They'll have to scrimp some more, dump the TV. Mang Pedring can disconnect it, for all she cares. But first *that* woman has to go. She has brought this bad luck and it's growing worse—now where's that Noland? Her stomach tightens as she thinks of her son's awed ministrations over the unwanted guest. She empties the water from the final rinse. It floods everyone's feet and splashes the dog, who chases the flow and laps at a puddle before rolling in it for a morning bath.

13

Look, lady, look. Noland passes a plate of bread over the sleeping woman's head, then the McDonald's bun under her nose, but she's still, so still. He pulled the mat slightly after Elvis left; he couldn't help himself. Her face must catch the glow seeping through the cherub on the roof. Now he can make out the curve of her brow, her hair. He lifts a lock, she shifts. He drops the hair and holds his breath, but she grows still again. He comes closer.

Her lids flutter. She knows it's him.

She tilts her chin. Toward him. See, she knows. Angels know like that.

Her nose delights him, its bridge so high. He touches his own.

Her breath quickens on his cheek. He draws back.

But you can't sleep and sleep. It's morning.

He looks up. Maybe the shaft of light from the cherub will hit her eyes, angel to angel. Then she'll wake up and morning will break in the whole hut. Light to light.

She senses not light but warmth on her cheek: someone's breath, the cadence of a silent tale.

Maybe he wanted to shoot you too. He shot the nice man. Germinio de Vera, his name. He was eating a pork bun. Behind your taxi. Slumped on his wheel. I saw. You saw. The boy rehearses the story he'd tell her, if he could speak. He rehearses the kinship. We saw. Together. You afraid? I was.

She groans. The breath is so close, like a kiss, like something she's been searching for all her waking life. But awake, will she truly see, or hear, or feel the awaited kiss? Isn't it sweeter now, in sleep when she can trust even the strange, when surrender is as inevitable as helplessness?

The woman breathes back at the face of the boy. She's no longer afraid. The boy breathes in return. Neither does he fear, kneeling like this, his face almost touching hers. Up in the roof, the cherub smiles at the two heads caught by a little pool of light.

14

Lights are useless in the day, a trying-too-hard magic that makes the stars look garish, so the lantern twins turn off the power in the stall. This means less hassle from the wire-man, who will come walking past anytime now to check whether they owe him more. Vic and Vim are particular about their business, so they're back at work even if Vim is scared—too many questions from the police. The twins have made lanterns all their lives, and their father before them and his own father too. They're proud of their trade. They polish each little shell before making a star.

One hundred and seventy-six little pieces make up a small star. Like life, the twins' father used to say when he was alive. You polish each part, you put it together, you light the whole thing. You have a right to shine like everyone else and make the world a little brighter, even here.

Here is the slums where three generations of their family have lived. Every now and then the government threatens eviction, relocation they call it, too risky here, they say. Every now and then a child dies under the train, on the tracks, their playground. But relocation where? Some village too poor to buy lanterns. And relocation for whose benefit? For the eyes of city folk and tourists, their relief from the pests who clog traffic and make Manila dirty. No, not everyone can be polished to a clean shine. Certainly not the diseased mongrel that's sniffing at the shoppers and flicking its wet tail, much to their horror. The stall owners yell at the dog to get lost.

The intersection is back to normal again and more real in the day. Up and down the track, the wretchedness; parallel to it, the stars. And passing by, the procession of Mercedes and Pajeros sometimes stopping to relocate these shining things to where they rightfully belong, in heaven, perhaps to hang at its security window or in a fortified garden to complete the season's look.

Star and money change hands. How amazing this intersection, this quick meeting of star-maker and heaven-keeper. Sometimes someone gets a tip and maybe the angels up there blow their trumpets, indeed goodwill among men, but nothing can be louder than the irate tooting of horns to push traffic along.

It is the morning rush (but slowest) hour. Follow it, get on the highway, shut the ears to the carols and the eyes to the vendors and street kids, or the jeepneys missing each other by a hair's breadth, or just count each star lantern at each lamppost to ease the slow, slow crawl. Find some rest, maybe even the ocean breeze.

Finally the Baywalk along Roxas Boulevard. Elvis's short-time home, and Bobby Cool's. Both are smoking on a park bench close to the Manila Yacht Club. A herd of health buffs jog past and, still unsteady on his feet, a tourist ambles with a local date after a party that lasted till the morning, while the metro aides pace about their business of keeping the city clean. Their bright shirts are emblazoned with the name of the country's president, perhaps to proclaim how the highest official of the land keeps it clean by proxy. Or perhaps this is an insistence of mandate, constantly displayed like a T-shirt's brand name. The road is even more crammed with unmoving cars. The only semblance of peace is inside a hotel suite across the road where a traveling executive is just waking up for a breakfast meeting, or in a penthouse pool where a congressman is doing laps with his young starlet, or inside a four-wheel drive where the tinted windows hide a lawyer snoozing while his chauffeur navigates. How peaceful to be cut off from the frantic pace, and how cool. Heaven must be air-conditioned and God must not sweat. Nor must His angels be too ruffled, shuttling between solemnity and bliss only when the season calls for it.

On the bench, Bobby is breathing in Manila Bay and listening to his Walkman. He's freshly showered, his shirt still looking crisp despite the stains in the armpits. Elvis is similarly groomed, with a bunch of Noland's lanterns in his hand. A metro aide watches them, as absorbed as Bobby, who's shaking his body to the rhythm.

"Is it good?" the aide calls out.

Bobby nods, exaggerating his body movements: he's almost dancing, his gold crucifix swinging with the effort. The smiling aide copies him, body and broom in joyful unison. Elvis looks on, an outsider to the music. Bobby slaps him on the shoulder, relax Elvis, and beckons to the aide. "Have a listen," he says, sharing the earphones with the street sweeper, whose face breaks into an even bigger smile. The earphones get passed back and forth and both shake to the disco carol. Elvis looks away, rearranges the stars in his hand.

The phone rings. Bobby waves the aide away and takes the call. He slaps Elvis on the shoulder again. "C'mon, star delivery coming up." They cross the street, running around the cars that have revved back into action, rushing to some appointment they can't miss. The boy is clutching the stars to add to the client's five-star suite. Stars to convince the reception desk of a legitimate delivery.

A few minutes later, Bobby Cool steps out of the hotel. He's looking more crisp, more cool, the carols set in his Walkman, the dollars secure in his pocket.

15

It's midday and still she sleeps. Noland frets about her stillness. He can't see the massive swelling hidden by her blond hair but the purplish bruise on the left temple is obvious now, and the tinge of purple too on the cheek. So still, so still. He keeps fretting. The peaceful exchange of breath earlier was only a brief lull. Again he passes his hand close to her nostrils and mouth to check the flow of air, as if the rise and fall of the chest can't assure him enough.

Her cheeks twitch, perhaps sensing the almost laying on of hands. He reads her every movement, and imagines it when there's none. She lets out a groan or maybe it's a word, an English word of course, incomprehensible but meant for him, the boy believes. But she's quickly still again. He closes his eyes, his whole body listening. He'll eavesdrop on her dreams, they'll have a conversation there, she'll talk to him, he'll respond. He will speak.

The angels wait. On the roof, the spot of light on the cherub's brow has grown, as if its brain were now infused by some lucent thought. Saint Michael and Saint Raphael, and even his fish, are also glowing. The midday sun betrays the hut's holes and gashes, this life not quite stitched at the seams, but the betrayal is welcome. Even the angel patching the door to the wall lets in more of the morning, so the lost trumpet seems to have been found, perhaps to amplify the conversation below. What is it that they hear?

Two tongues, two voices. Pilipino and English, a boy and a woman conspiring.

"*May alam akong kuwento . . .*" "I know a story . . ."
"So do I . . ."   "*Ako rin . . .*"
"*Kuwentong di mo alam . . .*" "A story you don't know . . ."
"Nor do you know mine." "*Di mo rin alam ang akin.*"

The boy sketches the unknowable in his head, extending his comic strip from before, revising the cosmic.
Four stars in the sky.
Big angel falling from the fourth star.
Small angel flying from the first star.
Small angel on the pavement, arms open and waiting for the fall.

16

Nena and her laundry ride home in Noland's cart with a pail of water. She wants to scold her son but loses heart. Instead she complains bitterly about how her only client was hijacked. "I'll wash the last lot tomorrow—the last lot, would you believe? . . . But who'd want to hire a lame washerwoman? . . . And I worked so hard. . . ." She's about to speak again but shuts her mouth.

The cart skirts puddles and dog turds, and Mikmik

and her gang blowing trumpets at their ears, asking after Noland's "dwarf stars." The nine-year-old bully is surprised they don't get a rise from "the witch"—she's not even looking at us? But mother and son keep their faces down, afraid the whole track will know about their guest, will see the truth in their eyes.

"You must throw that TV out."

Never, the boy protests. You love it.

"We can't afford it now."

The boy makes faces, uses gestures to explain his big plan. I'll sell more lanterns, I'll go back to the dump soon, more usable garbage there, people get new things for Christmas, and of course more bottles to sell.

"You know the police have been asking questions around here?"

Noland feels the need to pee, he has to pee. The ground trembles, then the rumble of machinery. Quickly Noland pushes the cart to the side, nearly bumping against Mang Pedring with his bag of tools. It's like being in a wind tunnel when they're caught this close to the passing train. Their clothes whip about, as if escaping from their bodies to hitch a ride to where there are houses with brand-new televisions and proper tables for a meal. Sometimes Noland wonders what would happen if they just took the train and never got off. Then there'd be no need for houses.

When they reach the hut, Noland leaves his mother at the door and runs to the back to relieve himself. The black creek wakes up, makes small ripples then is still again. He shivers; his shorts are wet. At the door, his mother detains him. "No, hang these first." She stretches the job, rummaging through the laundry, pretending to search for the perfect piece and the matching peg. Soon the washing lines look like flapping riggings of the hut, running from its roof to the wire fence. At the other side, the highway.

She doesn't want to go in, doesn't want to deal with that "bad-luck woman" sleeping on her mat. She wants to talk about *her* to Noland, about all the trouble that she's waking up in their lives. But how to speak of stories that must sleep? How to break this silence between them? She wants to scold, but all she does is ask, "Is she awake?"

17

Helen knocks on the door with a bowl of chicken soup. She calls out to Nena and Noland, but the hut is silent. She shrugs her shoulders, mumbles that they're probably out, and returns to her hut across the track. Her husband, who takes the bowl from her, is collecting money from the line of video buffs. This afternoon, he's showing *Bad Santa,* a deviation from the usual local films but perfect for the season. One mother who's with her three-year-old wants to know if it's a good idea for her daughter to see Santa bad, or if it's a good idea to make Santa bad in the first place.

"Don't worry, he's not really bad, just naughty, and it's a very, very funny film—watched it several times myself," Mario says, while sipping the soup. "Hoy, Helen," he calls out to his wife, "this is really good, plenty of ginger. I love ginger." He pushes the mother and child inside, mumbling, "I'm having my second helping. Don't worry, you'll like it too—that Santa's a hoot." He looks forward to his running translation and commentary as the film plays, well after he finishes this soup. "Hoy, Helen, play a cartoon first, one of those shorts."

At the window, Helen rolls her eyes to heaven. "Mario, you shouldn't be eating something that's meant for our neighbor."

"You and your nosy neighboring. It will get you into trouble one of these days."

"Nena's lost her only customer." She sighs, imagining her poor neighbor's "ugly legs" that she always tries to hide, and the boy's silence. They always make her sigh.

"Not your problem. I'm sad for her too but she's unreliable, slow washing, always sick, work delayed. Of course any client will find someone new." He's stuck into the chicken leg now.

"You have a stone heart, you know that?"

"Ay, Helen, I'm just practical. These times you have to be."

"She's acting funny. I've never seen her this distressed, this quarrelsome. Maybe because of last night, ay we're all afflicted by that—that—"

"Of course, she's the queen of misery."

"But this morning was different, she's even more—I wonder if they're okay, what with that shooting. I hope her son wasn't there, I hope—"

"You and your hope—but I'm not going to argue."

"You're a man with no conviction, no balls!" And Helen slams the window shut.

"No, I'm a peaceful man so I won't rise to your bait," he murmurs to himself, gnawing each chicken bone clean.

18

Kentucky Fried Chicken and a huge bottle of Coke. Elvis is stuffing himself with the feast. He's naked, running from the table to under the sheets, television remote in one hand, a heaped plate in the other. There's a Bugs Bunny rerun on screen: he's being chased by Elmer Fudd with his shotgun. Bugs hops onto the carrot patch, uprooting a carrot at each hop. Elmer aims— "You wascal wabbit!"—but Bugs confuses him by throwing carrots in the air, juggling them. Elmer fires but hits only a carrot, then another, and another. By the time Bugs is safe underground, he has only one carrot top left. "Oh well, at least there's dessert." He smirks, munching away.

Elvis giggles, copies Bugs's facial attitude and rabbit voice, "Oh well, at least there's dessert," and starts on the chicken. Then, as an afterthought, he yells, "Oh man, where dessert?"

"Ach, mein Gott, what big appetite you have, Elvie," a man calls out from the shower, laughing. "To better eat you, my dear," he responds to his own remark, laughing even louder.

"No Elvie, shit man—Elvis, okay?" the boy yells back.

"And what big voice you have—to better—better sing you, my dear," and he giggles. "Ach, water gut, Elvie, come."

"No, we finish."

"I buy you dessert, gut sweet."

"No, finish now, okay?"

"I give you dollar, more—"

"How more?"

"Ten—"

"Cheap—hundred—"

"What! Fifty—"

"No bargain, I give you gut, gut time." The boy imitates the other's accent. "Hundred—"

"Ach, you baddie boy, Elvie. Okay come, water very gut."

Elvis is silent. He's surprised the German took his call. He didn't want him to, but what the hell. He stops arguing over his name, and gives up on the food, the TV.

"Hundred okay, so I wash my Elvie nice."

The boy looks his naked body over in the mirror. He looks down there, rubs it, while finishing his Coke. Now he's ready. He opens a palm toward his reflection, mouthing "Gimme five!" and goes into the shower.

19

How to make a star. Noland thinks it, draws it. He fills his notebook with stars of all sizes, all shapes, prospecting beyond the usual five points, but then returns to the old model. He hears himself speak in his head, encouraging his hand.

"Star." He fills the whole page with a five-pointed star.

"One light." He encircles the first point.

"Two lights." He encircles the second too, and so on. When he's done the lot, he hears his verdict. "A star has five lights. *Only* five."

He has been drawing since lunch and has even forgotten to hide the notebook where he figures out the world and why she hasn't woken. He and his mother ate the guest's breakfast, even the burger. Now he touches her foot, very slightly—she's burning. He looks to his mother anxiously. She hasn't spoken since they went in after hanging out the laundry. She checked on the sleeping woman, touched her arm, her forehead, wrung her hands. Infection, what if she has an infection *there*, after—or the blood loss must have gone to her head, made it hot, this fever, ay, *Dios ko*.

Nena is on the floor, boiling water on the stove. The Amerkana needs a hot sponge to make her sweat, to get that fever down. Then she hears the sudden movement and her son's intake of breath—the white woman has sat up, she's beginning to scream! Nena runs to her and clamps a hand over her mouth, terrified that the whole track will hear. She holds her, keeps holding her until she settles back to her dream, while Noland squats at their feet, eyes fixed on the women clinging to each other, vowing he'll love them forever.

20

At five-thirty, Noland is outside Quiapo church, sent on an urgent errand. His mother could only think, herbs from Quiapo. No one will die in her house, no one will die on her again, not even a stranger! He holds the piece of paper to give to the vendor. Nena set this list on his palm then closed it, murmuring an invocation of faith: "This will work, this must work."

Noland is swept up by the rush hour. Crowds frantic

to get home are making detours for commerce and God, and for every other need.

"How much for the fish? You're sure it's as fresh as it looks? How much for the flowers? I want a bunch for my altar. How much for this Child Jesus? He's perfect for my manger. Oh, this little Bethlehem is cute. How much for fortune telling? Your cards aren't accurate. How much for these mahogany seeds? The packet says, 'Tried and tested, an effective cure for diabetes, arthritis, rheumatism, ulcer, asthma, high blood, stomach pain, cough, menstruation, cancer.' Are you sure? Oh, but how expensive."

From the market around the corner, through Plaza Miranda, and now outside the church, Noland has eavesdropped on all the bargaining. Its urgency is irresistible. It must really be Christmas. Everyone wants more, hopes more. Earlier, as he cut across the plaza, the Christmas ornaments made him dally awhile. A stage was being decked for the Christmas Eve celebration— the angel was the largest he's seen yet, and it was a lantern too, an angel lantern—and they're still working on her, look. If he cranes his neck now—the boy sidesteps the crowd, trying to get a view of the lantern again. It's being hoisted to the top of the stage. He hops up and down. He is too young to know about another stage that made this plaza a landmark. In 1972 a political rally was bombed here. The bombing "justified" a dictator's years of martial law.

Finally, he finds a little rise on the pavement. He steps up; he can almost see the angel's head.

"Hoy, out of the way!" someone scolds.

It's the "religious" vendor asking Noland to make room for her customer, who's haggling over the going rate for novenas. Her son is very ill and she can't afford the surgery, but maybe a miracle.... She's rushing to her third job, so she's contracting the vendor to do the prayers for her. "And pray to the Black Nazarene too, it might work this time, it's Christmas, you know."

This will work, this must work. Noland suddenly hears his mother's words. How could he get distracted! He clutches the list, thinks of his own angel at home, her fever. He walks around the church, examining the stalls of bottles and packets. Root, bark, fruit, leaf, sap, even things he cannot identify, all packed for every ailment in the world. Here where wallets are thin or empty, it is faith that cures, it is deprivation that makes miracles.

The boy stares hard at the list but can't divine its intent. He has yet to learn how to read the squiggles:

Para nakunan. Panlinis. For miscarriage. For cleaning.

Tentatively he moves toward two vendors sorting their wares, taps one on the shoulder and holds out the piece of paper.

One of the women grabs it without looking up. "What's this?" She frowns. "Is this an 'n' or an 'm'— *nakunan* or *makunan*?" Is this "for miscarriage" or "to miscarry." Then she realizes it's a boy before her. "What, your mother sent you to buy this? *Hesusmaryosep,* Jesus-MaryJoseph, your mother has no *delicadeza"*—no delicacy of manner, no propriety. "Who'd send her son on an errand like this! Have a look at this, have a look." She shows the list to the other woman. "It says, 'to miscarry,' doesn't it? Hoy, we don't sell that!" The woman quickly covers a row of bottles labeled *pamparegla,* to induce menstruation. The herb is discreetly traded outside the church that condemns abortionists to hell.

"Go away, boy! How dare you come to us!" she spits.

Noland escapes, perplexed by her anger. But there's no time to find out why. Quickly he's swept in the surge of the faithful, into the church.

21

It is Quiapo's center, this Black Nazarene that has literally come through fire. It was blackened by a shipboard fire on the journey from Acapulco to Manila in 1606, but by the grace of God was saved. How miraculous, like all the tales of salvation that brought the wretched *indios* to their knees for nearly four hundred years, much to the approbation of the Spanish conquistador. Let these "Indians" hope for heavenly redemption, not a country's liberation.

Centuries later, the faithful still pin their hopes on it. They too will come through suffering with the intercession of this burnt Christ, who is looking up though weighed down by His cross. They too are looking up from their knees, to Him. Their hopeful gaze has fixed this Christ in His suffering. His cross is not the world's iniquity, as is preached, but its hope.

You were born poor and suffered like us but rose to glory, so surely we can too, we must. How wearying to have the world demand this of anyone, how exhausting to be God. But humanity is wired to hope, aim higher than its height, and pity the man or god assigned to fulfill it. Inside the church, the man-God is flanked by the oldest stories of restitution in stained glass: His birth in a manger, *Gloria in Excelsis Deo,* and His glorious resurrection, or is it the final judgment?

The late sun is streaming through the glass; the candles are lit. The altar is a spectacle. The faithful look up and up. Not Noland, though. His gaze is fixed lower down, on the angels guarding the Black Nazarene, for whom he has no time.

Noland likes his Jesus white, his angels bright, as they are in the ads and on Christmas cards. So he crosses himself before the winged guardians instead, surveys their clean robes, their golden hair. He wonders about their feet. How are they shod? He imagines his own angel asleep at home and is overwhelmed by inspiration that's hardly divine. He rushes out of the church, checking his pocket for remaining cash and the bottle of herb that another vendor sold him without asking questions. He's hatching more domestic stratagems. Like all the faithful this boy hopes, but it hasn't occurred to him to kneel, to pass on hope as a burden on anyone's shoulder.

His mother stopped going to church years ago, so he conjured his own cathedral. He longed for angels; he found them. He wished for stars; he made them.

It's nearly dark when he reaches Central Market at the other end of Quiapo. He walks the dimly lit corridors of plastic flowers, beaded dresses, fake designer jeans, then finally finds where the housedresses are sold. He fondles them—how soft, how bright. The vendors are impatient.

"What would you like? Is it for your mother, a Christmas gift? What's her size?"

No answer from the boy. He's looking for blue, the right blue.

A hundred pesos for small, a hundred and sixty for large. He checks his pocket. Twenty pesos, that's all. It doesn't stop him. He keeps searching for a good ten minutes. The vendors are not convinced. They drive the street kid away.

22

The only light comes from the television playing a Mexican soap opera with Pilipino subtitles. Nena stares at the reunion of her favorite lovers but can't quite follow the passionate repartee. She keeps shifting and glancing at the sleeping American, muttering that she can't stay here. When *City Flash* comes on, she freezes. The face of the "salvaged" journalist Germinio de Vera fills the screen. He wears a puzzled look, the same one that wondered why on earth he thought the palm of a child was as small as a star, as small as a country, as small as hope. Did he save this thought for broadcast to more than seventy million viewers tonight?

Salvaged doesn't mean "saved" in this part of the world, which has turned an English word inside out to reveal the dark interior, the deadly heart. The news speculates that Germinio de Vera was salvaged for exposing a senator's "friendship" with a famous *Jueteng* King, the godfather of illegal gambling. Perhaps the senator's election campaign was funded by this generous personage? As a consequence the senator looks the other way when the king-maker flaunts his mansions and fast cars and three mistresses maintained by the masses' faith in numbers dreamt up or rumbled for luck. But the journalist pushed his own luck further, throwing the deadly card on the table with the question: Was the senator the *Jueteng* King himself? The answer was a speedy salvaging, on a motorcycle.

The news cuts to the reporter Eugene Costa, trying to wrangle an interview from the man himself. Senator G.B. "Good Boy" Buracher is surrounded by children singing "Silent Night." He's hosting a Christmas party for orphans at a hospice. Two girls aged six and five are on his knees, perplexed by all the attention. His body-guards block the reporter. The news cuts again to the intersection, then to a speeding Pizza Hut motorcycle and back to the *City Flash* anchorwoman asking, "But who is the Pizza Hut man?"

Then just as in life, which can't stay singular or still, the news moves on to the joint exercises of the Philippine and the United States military in their common fight against terrorism. At efficiently stage-managed press conferences, the countries' respective presidents affirm current bilateral relations and "our long history of friendship." But the camera is fickle. It cuts to a veteran activist asking whether this paves the way for the revival of the U.S. military bases, which were shut in 1992.

Face after face, news after news, life after life, but Nena sees only her son's face evoking another from an earlier time. This is not a solemn face, though, but one fraught with query and puzzlement, with cares more numerous than the stalks of rice he planted long ago, as numerous as the stars watching over them, turning them to gold.

23

It whimpers, then is still. It does not know what hit it or whose hand dealt the blow. A dog cannot query its fate. It just dies. Elvis can't take his eyes off it, dragged back to the store by Mang Gusting. He shuts his eyes. He can't escape the last hiss of life when the head is severed from the neck. Can anyone die twice? He's sure he hears a final-final expiration. He feels his own neck, at the jugular where the pulse is undeniably still there—or is it?

What a waste of so much Kentucky Fried Chicken. As he retches his way to Noland's hut, he assures himself he's only cleaning his insides. The German was overly generous. His affection stretched for two hours under the shower. He's sore. The German got his money's worth, every cent of his one hundred dollars. Elvis checks the bill in his pocket. It's crisp and clean.

Close by Mikmik and her gang sing carols from hut to hut. The girls are bursting with Christmas cheer and prank, jumbling up lyrics, making them wicked, giving them oomph. They rev up with the traditional carol:

> *Ang pasko ay sumapit*
> *Habang ang mundo'y tabimik*
> *Ang araw ay sumapit*
> *Ng Sanggol na dulot ng langit.*

> *Christmas has come*
> *While the world is peaceful*
> *The day has come*
> *For the Child gifted by heaven.*

Then they revise it:

Ang pasko ay kumapit
Sa mundong masungit
Ang araw ay sumabit
Sa bulsang ubod ng buwisit.

Christmas latched itself
Onto a cruel world
The day derailed itself
In a pocket of bad luck.

Up and down the track, the children are condemned for sacrilege, blasphemy, and consigned to the devil's lair. Hah, that's what you get for leaving a daughter with a father who can't run a store and, worse, can't even be faithful. So what would he know about raising a girl?

Mikmik's mother has worked as a maid in Hong Kong for six years now. The neighbors envy Mang Gusting's Hong Kong dollars but not his domestic lot. His wife sent money for a store, then a karaoke to draw more customers, who only sang and drank each night on credit. And Micaela, who demands to be called Mikmik now, has grown up an impossible handful, giving everyone a reason to blame the absent mother and the incapable father.

What is it like to be incapacitated by longing? An empty bed, a daughter's brooding; the ache in the loin, the dent in the heart. In the first year, he cried each time his daughter cried herself to sleep. In the second, he went to the back of his store at midnight, read his wife's letters, and watched the cockroaches feast on his cum. In the fourth, when the karaoke machine was bought, he sang with his friends and watched the women, especially Lisa and her pulsing throat when she reached for the high notes. Much later, he took Lisa to the back of the store, but not to sing. Some heard her cry out, or so they say, thus the "oh-oh" tag to her name. But that's over now. Everything passes—the years, the preoccupations, and the affections. This Christmas, his wife did not send any money, not even a greeting card. He suspects she found out about his affair. One of her friends probably wrote her and dumped on him. Such things happen in this neighborhood.

"Hi, *handsama*," Mikmik greets Elvis with her limitless bravado, mixing up the word "handsome" and *sama*, "bad." Her gang of younger girls blow their Christmas trumpets.

"Hi, bee-yoo-tee," Elvis tosses back, even if his spirit isn't quite all there. Thank God it's dark so she can't see he's turned white. He heads to the public pump to wash off the smell of retch. Bobby said there's another job late tonight—fuck you, Bobby. He pumps the water onto his head, his face. He's dripping when he gets to Noland's hut.

"Gotta towel?"

Noland and his mother are at the Amerkana's feet; she's still asleep. Nena shushes the dripping boy, but Noland is ready with a rag for his friend, gesticulating with worry—she's very sick.

What do you know about sick? He's sore, queasy, exhausted, and he can't get the dog off his mind, that last hiss. "So, we selling?" He rubs his hair dry, and his cheeks for color. He can feel how white he's become, but these people can't see, of course, caught up with that woman. "No? No selling?" No one can see because no one has ever looked. "I'm going then."

"Good," Nena grumbles, but Noland gestures for him to wait as he gathers his wares in a bag; no need for the cart. No time to make more stars today. She's sick, you see. He's torn between going with his friend and squatting at the feet of that woman like some slave dog. Elvis can see that.

The shadows in the hut grow still. The heart of the Christmas tree flickers. All are dying for an ending.

"Let that devil boy go, Noland," Nena scolds but the boys are soon out the door. She sighs, lays a hand on the white woman's brow.

At the intersection, Elvis is sullen. He squats under the giant stars, mouth tightly drawn. The stall owner eyes him suspiciously. Bad temper, bad luck. "Hoy, don't block my customers," he scolds, waving him away.

Bobby looks him over too, sniffs him. "You smell funny—glad I brought these," tossing him a bag of fresh clothes. "Tonight's special."

Elvis simply shrugs and receives the business accessories, including a cell phone, the whispered details, and his share of the German loot, in pesos of course. Bobby never tells him how much he collects. Never mind, he won't know about those two extra hours either. They're even.

"See you there, don't be late." The pimp is off to set up the night.

Under the blinking lights, Elvis is red, green, and yellow, and different. Noland notices, and touches his arm. Elvis flinches. No, red, green, and yellow, and sad. Noland rearranges the drooping cap. Elvis shrugs, spits out an expletive. When they *do* see, he can't bear it.

Suddenly he laughs, a hard note in Noland's ears. "Okay, Noland, let's conquer!" He grabs a handful of stars then is off, charging at the traffic.

As they dispatch the stars, they stray from the intersection, farther from Mang Gusting's store. The boy is perfect again after several turns of his cap, these revolutions of mood and luck. What luck this relocation of the heart. He is saved from the smell of dog barbecue. At Mang Gusting's, the karaoke party is in full swing. The beer flows with Christmas carols and Mikmik has lit up a string of firecrackers. But her father remains sober. Whatever made him think that Lisa's pulsing throat was smooth and graceful? Of course, her notes are still the highest of the singing lot, untouched by any man's affection or disaffection. What luck that disaffection is unknown to a mother's charges in Hong Kong. Those two little girls have doctors for parents and a Filipina amah who loves them like her own.

24

Nearly two hours before midnight and the stars have descended. Now sprouting from buildings and dripping from trees, lights and more lights glitter along Ayala Avenue, which has never known the pliers of the wire-man Mang Pedring. Noland beams at Elvis. It's like he has died and gone to heaven.

A change of heart, a change of scene. Heaven has relocated itself, and Noland is making blissful noises in his throat. Almost words, Elvis imagines. Earlier he slipped his friend a *balato,* a gift of four hundred pesos, because he said he'd scored a deal, though he won't talk about it. Two extra hours in the shower for a cool hundred dollars—ah, he'd outbargained that stupid German.

A warm feeling crept through his chest as Noland's mouth fell open. That's it, all trace of sullenness dislodged by a feel-good flush. Elvis was back at the wheel, navigating with ease as he extended the gift. "Why don't you come with me and splurge? I'm off to the shopping heart of the city."

Noland hesitated but was swept off his feet by Elvis's stories about those lights and other possibilities. *What if?*

"Told you, didn't I?" Elvis beams at his friend's awe. They're now a jeepney ride away from the intersection. Elvis explains how easy it is for Noland to catch a ride home. He's shown him the route, pointed out the jeepney to take. "No rush, it's midnight shopping. Buy your mother something nice for Christmas."

Noland fondles the bills, gets more inspired.

"You sure you don't have holes in that pocket?" Elvis asks, assessing the other's rag of a shirt with a Spider-Man print. He should have told him to change. "Keep your hands around your money. Easy to lose it in this shopping madness."

But how do I go in there? Noland's heart fills up with the immense size of Glorietta Mall and its implications. When Elvis said let's go "mall-ing," Noland looked perplexed and his friend laughed. "It's shopping or window-shopping, eating, etc., etc., getting into the grind like everyone else. An expedition!"

Noland has never been to a mall. He heard about it from the kids in the other slum where they used to live. It's so big with so many corridors leading to so many shops with everything that anyone can buy and eat. The choices will make you dizzy, the corridors will get you confused, get you lost.

"Just follow the crowd, you'll be fine. Or ask the guard over there."

Noland flinches at the mention of the guard.

"Okay, I'll lead you in, walk around a bit, but I have to meet Bobby somewhere around here, so I can't stay long." He looks at the fake Rolex that's too big for his wrist. Somewhere around here is the condominium of a Chinese businessman who's expecting an overnight. Bobby said to look "expensive," so he brought him the bag of imitations: Elvis had changed into Lacoste, Nike, and Rolex, but it's the same New York cap. I ♥ NY. Didn't the Amerkana say so?

"C'mon, then." He leads Noland by the hand, murmuring, "I think we should buy you a shirt," but a shirt is the last thing on Noland's mind. He imagines corridors and corridors of housedresses. With four hundred pesos plus the lantern sale in his pocket, anything's possible. But inspiration falters as they walk in. Near the entrance shoppers haggle for colorful gift boxes and designer perfumes on sale.

Why buy empty boxes that cost a dozen kilos of rice each? Why have a lady spray you for the price of more than a year's supply of rice? Of course there's the little box that she wraps up for you. Noland scratches his head.

The shoppers clutch their bags tighter as he stares at the thousand-peso bills laid on the counter until Elvis drags him away, whispering, "Noland, you don't stare at money here—you want us to get into trouble?" He tips his cap at the frowning sales attendant. "Just looking-looking, miss."

They walk on, Noland oh-ing and ah-ing in his head over this magnitude of Christmas spirit, the lights more glorious than what Elvis promised, the stars and angels all colors, sizes and shapes, and the din of carol and chatter leaving him breathless. Here is a church with richer altars, where masses offer a full range of intent, from joyful to anxious consumption.

They follow the faithful, lingering here and there for Noland's sake. Elvis is looking at his watch, Noland is ogling the display window of a bookstore where angels float, hanging from barely visible strings. He smiles at the shimmering creatures with golden hair, golden wings, and golden trimmings on their silk costumes. All with tall noses and looking serious, perhaps because they're guarding books. Under an angel's gaze are three little books arranged strategically to inspire each other: *101 Bathrooms*, *101 Living Rooms*, and *Finishing Touches*. Good thing Noland can't read. How to imagine a hundred and one bathroom options when for him it's the creek beside the hut.

Suddenly he jumps at the sound of orchestrating phones. He turns around. Three shoppers are intent on their palms. Elvis rolls his eyes to heaven.

A far-off century may suspect an epidemic of obsessive-compulsive palm reading, but this is only the new world texting, reading messages, and viewing photos. Thank God for efficient intimacies here, where most of the shopping rolls on dollars sent home by millions of overseas Filipino contract workers and migrants. The Filipino heart travels with an unflinching sense of duty. When the body is unable to return, the dollar flies back, or the beloved comes home on a little ring, a little beep. Back to where Christmas shopping must go on, where shoppers will never know how to freeze in winter and loneliness, or how to be raped by the employer from whom all the dollars flow.

Ignorance is bliss. The mall is busy, so life can only be prosperous.

Suddenly another ring. Elvis makes a big show for Noland's sake, naturally hand to ear as if the little gadget were born with him. It's Bobby tracking him down. "Of course I'm here, just across the road—okay, over and out." He fusses with his cap and clothes. "Gotta go, Noland—no, you'll be okay. Listen, if you keep following all those people, you'll get to Landmark, where you can buy anything and cheaper too, and I showed you where to take the jeepney, didn't I? Don't worry, you'll be okay, it's easy." But Noland won't let go of his hand.

"Remember, I showed you the jeepney route that goes all the way to your street, or close to it anyway—and buy yourself a shirt, okay?"

Noland is still holding onto him, for a moment his lifeline, this boy who looks strange and rich in his fake glory, noosed by a line too short, where the knot tightens at the end.

DECEMBER 21

25

Dinner is pork buns and Coke at 2 a.m. Nena queries Noland's rich takeaway at every mouthful. "Where did you get this, and the shirt, and the money? Did you sell all your lanterns?" She's more anxious about her son's bag of shopping, which he's trying to hide. "You didn't steal, did you? That Elvis didn't get you into some scrap again, did he? Is this why you're so late?"

Elated, Noland isn't listening. He is quickly beside his guest, checking for fever, catching his breath. He did not take the jeepney. He walked under the dripping fairy lights in his new shirt with the same words as on Elvis's cap: I ♥ NY. Fifteen pesos from the bargain box. He likes the big red heart, much bigger than the cap's.

"Where's he having Christmas anyway?" Nena asks, offhand. Perhaps she knows something about "that devil boy," perhaps not. After all, questions are like expletives sometimes, a mere impulsive twitch with no wish for answers. "Come to bed, Noland, she'll be okay."

He wants answers, but can't ask for them. He wonders about his friend who never runs out of money and never volunteers anything about himself. He wonders about the kind man who bought his star two nights ago and told him to keep the change, and the wondering stabs at his heart. He wonders what's wrong with his still sleeping guest and whether the bottle from Quiapo will make her well and when she will wake up.

He prefers home to the streets now, knowing she's here, that she might be awake. The thought always quickens his heart and pulse, pushes his feet into a sprint. His mother notes he does not even look at her when he walks in, heading straight to the white woman, squatting at her feet, watching over her before he does anything else. She resents his attention but doesn't have the heart to stop him, or maybe her heart is no longer whole for this. Once it broke because of this very same attitude of watching.

He came home earlier to deliver the herb. Nena worried endlessly about how she could give it to the Amerkana when she was asleep and what if she made a scene if she woke her, what if she screamed again, what if the whole neighborhood found out, but what if she never woke up?

For Noland at the mall, *what if* was all light and lightness. Ah, those stars, those angels. He walked, gazed, lingered, long after Elvis had gone. One display window perplexed him: two Christmas ball gowns flanked by stars without the usual finish. Just glittering wires, bones of a star. The lightbulb was naked, the heart exposed.

But why hide the heart anyway? A little trick for the eye, a subtle camouflage is enough in the hut. Noland's handmade tree proves this. Long after dinner, the candle still flickers inside the milk can, inside the bamboo. He raises a hand to stop his mother from blowing it out. He can't sleep, he won't. He's still at her feet, listening to the ebb and flow of her breath, checking for fever. What if.

Nena cheers up her boy. "She woke up and asked for water...I gave her the herb...don't worry, I think the fever's settling down...." Then just before she drifts off: "But she must go tomorrow...."

When all is still, Noland checks his shopping. Sliced bread, Milo and cheese, in precious little packets. Then two housedresses and a pair of slippers from the bargain box. One dress is red with black fishes, the other blue with red and white flowers. The slippers are also blue. There's also a cheap plastic curtain. It's a dull yellow, flowered too and opaque. Quietly he hangs it with laundry pegs to hide his guest, to keep her private and safe. Then he lays his hand on her brow to check for fever and, in a bold impulse, his head on her chest to check for life.

The woman dreams of a heaviness. She knows the weight of all the sobs of her life, but *this* is different. She wants it to stay, please stay. The boy stays long enough to hear enough, the one speech that truly gratifies.

26

In the still-dark morning Saint Raphael feels his fish twitch, wishing for a return to water. Saint Michael hopes to be free of his soot, to look more formidable. The Christmas angel despairs over the uselessness of her lungs, and wants a new trumpet. The cherub longs to fly down from the roof, try earth for a change. But they are set in their places and movement is made possible only by the passing train.

Do angels also aspire for things beyond them? If so, one can excuse humans who pray or pay for a wish, whichever is the realistic option. And in between, rest when possible. Be still again, be fixed in place. As the city prepares for the *Misa de Aguinaldo*, the pre-dawn Christmas mass, Noland begins to fall asleep. It's a restless sleep. He turns to the hidden guest. One arm makes a gesture toward her, then goes limp again. Maybe he's dreaming too soon. He hears:

Star-light, star-bright
Make-a-wish-a-wish-tonight.

The nursery rhyme is the ringtone of a cell phone. It plays from all the seven continents but no one picks up the call. It's the dream of the abandoned. The phone is unattended because everyone is out Christmas shopping.

The rhyme grows louder. It enters the hut, someone is calling the hut, but even here no one answers. Everyone is asleep, fixed in repose. The caller is persistent, then eventually gives up.

For a while, silence, then a soft light grows behind the plastic curtain. It grows bright, brighter. In his dream Noland sees it, recognizes it. He hears himself speak in his head. *I know a story you don't know.*

In the brightness, a silhouette rises. It sits up, its arms open. They become wings, they quiver, they stop. Again, fixed and still.

27

Everything is fixed and still in each box in a comic strip. But the pose in each box shifts from the previous one, and on it goes. Every story moves, even in a dream, or else there's no story at all.

So behind the plastic curtain, a silhouette rises.

It sits up.

Its arms open.

They become wings.

They flutter.

The silhouette flies through the plastic.

It hovers over the sleeping boy.

He wakes up.

He rubs his eyes.

It's an angel!

She hushes him.

She gathers him.

They tiptoe to the Christmas tree.

He touches her chest.

Her chest lights up.

She touches the tree.

Its heart lights up.

She points to this flickering light.

She whispers into his ear.

They shrink.

They fly into the heart of the tree.

They have many conversations.

Speech balloons from the tree.

Stories float around the hut.

Then the fog.

28

The 6 a.m. train zips past. The hanging stars dance in a fog. Rows of red and green flick their little paper tails. Farther up, a cherub slips in and out of the fog. She shuts her eyes again, opens them. Where is she, where is this? She feels the beginning of the query on her lips. Her eyes leave heaven and settle at her feet where a boy is staring. She stares back. He is out of focus.

He moves closer, a red heart out of the fog. I ♥ NY. Now she can see. The boy's eyes are open so wide that they fill his face, which is brown as a nut. His lips move slightly as if about to speak, and his rather large head covered by a mop of black inclines in the same attitude. *I am about to say.* But nothing. He is silent, solemn, yet she senses an intense yearning somewhere—is it in the eyes? It occurs to her that no one has ever looked at her like this.

It's a look that knows, but without the weight of history to frame the gaze. Yes, he knows about her, all of her from the day she was born, but this knowing now, this ultimate face to face, is what he trusts. The eyes say, tell me a story and it will be the only story that will matter. This is how she wants to be looked at.

He leaves her.

"Who? . . . Where?" The American tries again. She attempts to sit up, at least she feels she's sitting up, but she has barely moved. Her head, her stomach hurt. She fondles the blue housedress that she's wearing. The slippers at the foot of her mat are also blue. The smell of plastic fills her nostrils, and something stronger, like dead rats, decay—what is it? She doesn't know about the creek outside. She turns slightly. Her face touches the yellow curtain. She wants to lift it but her arm is too heavy. She searches for thoughts, for any inkling about who what where how, but her mind is empty, no there's a fog in there, no her mind's not even there. It's only her body that tells her she's here under the stars, and now under the gaze of the boy again. Her whole body hurts, her whole body isn't quite whole, it's missing something. What is it? Where am I? Lost in a fog, where everything is slow.

The boy has returned with two slices of bread with a yellow spread and a glass of something brown. What's it called? He motions for her to eat. She wants to, she's ravenous, but can't quite pick up the bread. He feeds her. It takes forever to finish the first slice. He watches, hardly blinking. I was right. Your eyes are blue.

29

Nena does her last laundry, and Helen commiserates. Nena keeps beating and wringing silently. Helen keeps up the loud sympathy. Thank God, Lisa is absent today, so they're spared a fight. "Hoy, Nena, I knocked at your door yesterday, I brought the chicken soup but no one was home. What a pity, it had plenty of ginger, and you love ginger, don't you? By the way, how's Noland? Haven't seen much of him. How are his lanterns? Hoy, come to the house for *Noche Buena,*" and on she talks about how she's preparing this Christmas Eve meal which Nena and Noland are welcome to share, yes, let's greet the birth of Christ together.

The other washerwomen and those waiting to fetch water keep their voices down at first but as the storytelling progresses, the pitch rises, the pace speeds up, the speculations and summations multiply like soap suds.

"It's Vim, one of the lantern twins. Bashed last night, maybe because he told the police everything. He saw the shooting, you know."

"*Dios ko,* our poor Vim, our poor foolish Vim, always wanting to do the right thing—"

"Never learns from his twin. Vic knows how to keep low, knows about life. Ay, poor brothers."

"Who would do such a thing to the kindest of men?"

"I'm scared."

"It's here, whatever it is—and it's Christmas too, ay, ay!"

"It's the Pizza Hut man—"

"No, don't say, don't say—"

"It's on *City Flash* all the time—"

"Could be a serial killer—"

"Oh no, don't say—"

"You know an Amerkana was also shot?"

"What?" everyone cries in unison.

All washing stops, and Nena's heart.

"Vim told the police there was an Amerkana, that she fell and just disappeared. Vim lost sight of her—he had run to help that poor guy in the car, then she was gone. But trust Vim to do the silly thing. Look what happened to him, and it's Christmas too."

In and out of the voices, the pump squeaks and grates, like some machinery cranking up the narrative and nerves.

30

Noland is hanging his mother's laundry, her last job. She's crouched inside the cart, her distress shifting between the pain in her legs and the news from the women. "She'll get us into trouble, she must go today. I said no police, no uniforms. Ay Noland, what will become of us? What will become of you?

"When you grow up, you will be a farmer like your father, but you will be better. You will own these fields of rice." Once Nena knew what would become of her son. She knew her wish by heart.

Star-light, star-bright
Make-a-wish-a-wish-tonight

"Watch how the stars watch the fields for you, Noland, for when the right time comes, because the stars know your name. Watch how the stars come so close to earth, as if they're descending on that hill over there. Those stars are angels guarding the land and the hearts that will always be true to it."

At four years old, Noland could not understand the story-wish, but he took the stars and angels to heart. He liked it when his mother's voice hummed with the crickets as he closed his eyes. It was a mother cricket's wish. "May your heart always be true, my son, like your father's and his father's before him," then she made the sign of the cross on him and herself. She believed in the grace of prayer then.

What will become of you? She has not asked this question in a long time and more so now, she dare not answer it, not even in her head. Nor has she spoken about her husband, lest they are returned to another story.

Noland hides his impatience. He wants to get back inside, to surprise his mother with this most beautiful thing, awake. He wrings a bedsheet with her. He pegs it onto the fence. It spreads like a white map. Through it he can see the highway traffic, now picking up. For the first time he feels that he too is going somewhere, finding his own route. He thinks of a blue housedress and blue slippers, and the Milo, of course. Milo's good. His chest swells with the knowledge that an angel was feeding from his hand.

"You've been very wasteful, Noland."

His poor mother can't understand, of course.

"Those dresses and things...the money, where did you get it? Ay-ay, what will I find out next?"

He squats before the cart, before his mother and her laundry, and takes her hands to his chest. Ah, this old habit, this conversation. Her son can speak in there and her hands can hear. His heart is true and she trusts it, but not this time.

"What trouble will you bring into the house next?"

It's eight in the morning. The boy wants to tell his mother about what awaits them inside. He wants to tell her stories about the street of lights and the mall of stars and angels, the thousands of pesos passing hands, the things to buy and eat that he can't even name, the piles and piles of clothes where he dug like all those desperate for something cheap but special, those without dollars from abroad who must still get on with the tradition of Christmas gift-giving. How he found the perfect housedresses there — do you like yours, Mother? I know you like red.

"I see you bought her slippers too."

The boy hears a strange note in his mother's voice. He's never heard it before. He's never heard jealousy. It perplexes his ear. She says yet almost asks, voice rising slightly at the finish, as if to confirm that the one not bought slippers is loved as much.

The mall, Mother, it's heaven. He wants to take her there, if only she could walk. If only his wooden cart would fit through the door. The guard would check it, as he checks all the bags, and send them away. And his poor mother wouldn't even dare to come close. She'd spot the uniform too soon.

31

Light is streaming in through the angels. The American looks up and around, her body bent so she doesn't hit the roof, her arms stretched out, catching the light from the cherub's brow and the brightness bisecting the angel at the door. She sees more light sneaking in through the holes and gaps, the seams of this oh-so-strange place. Where is this? One angel's fish grows a halo; another angel begins to glow. The light bounces on the ancient kerosene stove. The stars above are strung with light; their tails tickle her face. She's in a daze. Where am I?

She was hot when she woke up and a boy was feeding her, no, it was an old woman making her drink some bitter thing and she slept again or did she? And was there really a boy, a woman? Yes, she woke up drowning in hot fog and she crawled out of the plastic curtain and found her feet, then this—this magical shabby heaven that smells like it's rotting. She notes the badly dented television with a Christmas tree enthroned on it. Painted white and hung with tiny red and green stars, and gouged at the belly, exposed. This is what occurs to her at first glance. She puts her hand into the hole of the tree and finds a milk can. She peers at the melted candle inside.

Suddenly the door opens and the angel there folds in two for a second, then is whole again. The boy and the old woman have entered and quickly shut the door. So they're real after all. Both are staring at her. They see a giant, a white giant! She withdraws her hand from the tree, suddenly guilty, caught in a grievous act, like feeling up someone's insides.

The old woman is crouched on the floor, looking up at her. She crawls forward into a stream of light. It gashes her face, her blinking eyes. "Okay you?" she asks, pointing a finger at her.

The American steps back, uncertain. The finger is more accusing than concerned.

The boy hasn't moved but the woman crawls even closer. "Okay you?" she asks again, then, "Who you?"

The high-pitched voice is aggressive. The American doesn't know how to answer. "W-where—where am I?" she asks instead.

The woman taps her chest. "My house."

The guest feels like an intruder.

"Who you?"

The guest tries to squeeze an answer out of her head, but there's nothing there. She closes her eyes, hears the insistent "Who you? Who you?" at her feet. The woman has crawled closer.

"I—I—" The American sways weakly, then collapses before the boy gets to her. She hears the woman speak sharply to the boy in their tongue, surely against her, even as she helps her back to the mat.

Above, the stars grow fuzzy.

"Who you?"

The American attempts to declare herself, stammering through the "I" that feels like a coil of air making shapes in her mouth, except a name. She sees the word "who" flashing red inside her head. She hears someone sobbing. She hears it drag out of her mouth. "I—I don't know...."

32

Angels weep. He will remember this. They get hungry too, so weeping is all right. He watches his mother settle the weeping guest on the mat, her sharp demeanor now gone. "Okay, no-cry, no-cry," she croons instead.

"I—I don't remember...anything." The guest's voice rises in a panic.

"Sshh...shhh...." Nena feels the other's hands grip hers tightly, the nails digging in with every word.

"Some-something happened...something...."

Everything happened, that's why we're here. Nena feels the lump in her throat breaking, but she must settle her or else she'll start screaming again and everyone will find out. "Okay, no name. You know tomorrow, okay?"

The other woman nods, repeating, "Name...."

"Me, Nena. Son, Noland."

The boy nods wordlessly. She will always remember him squatting at her feet with that solemn stare. So son and mother. She thought Nena was an old woman. The streaks of gray, the hunched frame in a tattered housedress...so she can't walk? She tries to smile. "Noland, Nena."

"Yes, yes, me Nena, Pilipina."

"Pilipina...Philippines...."

Nena is excited. "Philippines you know, good, good. Philippines here, Manila here, my house here, you here, okay."

Okay, she's okay. The American closes her eyes tiredly. When she opens them again, Nena is still by her side and the boy is holding out a glass.

"Milo good," the mother approves. "Noland good boy."

"Good...thank you...."

They barely hear her; she's drifting off again. Nena reverts to Pilipino. "I told you she should go. And what's this curtain? Look, she's hot, she can't breathe. Her brain must breathe so she remembers, so she can go...soon." She quickly undoes the curtain, muttering, "Soon, soon."

Half asleep, the white woman murmurs, "You know me, Noland?" but the boy only stares.

"Sorry no talk, six years no talk...."

No talk? No one hears his thoughts where he knows everything. I know a story you don't know. I know you. I know your name. *Angel.*

She tries to reach for the boy, who offers his hand, but a whirring sound breaks the quiet. It's coming from above, outside. Instinctively they all look up. The hanging stars blur before the sick woman's eyes. The boy closes his own in the attitude of listening. Angel wings.

33

A Huey helicopter hovers over the intersection. The slums, the lantern stalls, the stars are whipped about, and so are the crowds below who have come out to look up and wave. The children are ecstatic. They've never seen anything this big and shiny fly this low and almost graze their lives. And look, there's a white man up there, about to land! Mikmik and her gang instigate contact, yelling, "Merry Christmas, Merry Christmas!" Other children instinctively join in. The pilot makes a thumbs-up sign to the man beside him. "Christmas spirit," he mouths.

Colonel David Lane doesn't welcome the gesture, abruptly making his own to the local flight lieutenant: Do a circuit of the track. He has grave doubts about this assignment. It's a civilian matter, for God's sake, but after 9/11 any American gets hurt or gets sneezed at in a foreign country and "terrorism" rears its ugly head. The Philippine government has approved this Huey tour, despite protests from local officials, overruled by "higher powers" upholding the Philippine-American friendship and the drawdown of ten million U.S. dollars for military assistance. "These slums go forever along the track," the Filipino escort behind Lane yells above the din. He's a veteran from Mindanao, his machine gun set for optimum visibility, as are the rocket pods. "Want us to cover it all, Colonel?"

David Lane shakes his head: just "a little tour" of the

slums, the embassy, then back to base. Once for him the base was 9/11. He was there the day after, so he went to Iraq. Then, in his heart, it felt right. But has he, in fact, done it wrong? When did the heart become a cog in a wheel that is now impossible to turn back?

Ambivalence. Ah, this scary thorn in the side, but how reassuringly human. And dangerously so for the trigger finger. It demands only conviction. An American life is at stake, so fly a combat helicopter to show we refuse to be terrorized. Part of operations, and he can't be accused of being unpatriotic, un-American. Always protecting our own. He orders the pilot to do another circuit.

Mang Gusting scolds his daughter: "Stop screaming your Merry Christmas!" That helicopter is a premonition, like the shooting, like the Pizza Hut man. Their lives will be turned upside down. Beside him the wire-man is wrapped in his own thoughts. What a beauty is this flying thing. He thinks of bigger planes, he thinks of war. So does Mario. He has seen enough war videos to know that a helicopter this close means trouble, and a white man in it means action, soon. Of course. Did the lantern twins not say an American was also shot? And she's missing. His wife Helen finds it hard to breathe, like the baby at her elbow. It's clutched tighter to its mother's breast, smothered by fear like Lisa's "oh-oh"; for once she's dumbstruck. Manang Betya crosses herself, thinking the end of the world is near, maybe after Christmas.

The Huey moves out into the city. In full combat gear

and burnished by the sun, it is a Christmas tinsel to contend with.

A vagrant sleeping on the pavement wakes up: is it landing on him? Around the corner, those lining up for a McDonald's breakfast jump at the ominous drone. Farther out along Roxas Boulevard, street kids are distracted from begging, shielding their eyes to see the beauty better. A businessman and his mistress sit up in bed, awed by the helicopter with a machine gun hanging out right at their hotel window, while in Starbucks below a junior executive texts a friend, *US abt 2 Lnd!*

It lands on the manicured lawns of the American embassy. The acacia trees hung with star lanterns bristle. American marines in an armored car look up. The consul has just received the latest brief about her probably shot, probably abducted compatriot. The woman's photo now appears on her computer screen, along with a story about the Pizza Hut man. A tiny Christmas tree winks absurdly on its heading.

Somewhere else a Pizza Hut manager argues with *City Flash* reporter Eugene Costa, on a stakeout to interview workers and clients.

"You can't accuse me of conspiracy to murder, you stupid meddler!"

"No, sir, I'm not accusing, sir, I'm asking."

"You mean 'interrogating'?"

"I don't interrogate, the police do that—I simply report, sir."

"Get your film crew out of here—I said get it out!"

34

Before his sleeping guest, Noland's eyes are still closed in the attitude of listening. It's out there flying. *They all know now, everyone knows.* His mother calls him; he opens his eyes. The beating of wings becomes the sound of a faraway helicopter again.

It has landed the second time in another territory, the Philippines' Villamor Airbase. Colonel Lane is welcomed by his Filipino counterpart, Colonel Romero. Under the still-churning Huey, the men salute each other, then shake hands with a more social heartiness. There's the usual slapping of the other's arm, like a manly support of the handshake. The cameras click, the films roll, the reporters angle for the right grab.

"Is this meeting about the *Balikatan* program, sir—or is it about the missing American? Do you think it's a hostage situation, like those that happened in the south—in Mindanao?"

"Do you believe the hostage crises in Mindanao were motivated by terrorism? Are you sure the Abu Sayyaf is a real terrorist group or is it a criminal gang? Is this why you've reinforced the *Balikatan* program, sir?"

"*Balikatan* means 'shoulder to shoulder'—but are you sure it's about our countries fighting the war on terror together? Isn't it about Washington paving the way to reopen the U.S. bases here? Are you getting nostalgic for the old days?"

Colonel Romero raises both hands diplomatically, as

if in surrender; he chooses his words with care. "The Philippines and the United States have always worked shoulder to shoulder. But right now, we're off duty. We're having our Christmas lunch, so if you'll excuse us." The two officers, who have only just met, walk away like old friends to a generous spread of Philippine delicacies, spirits, and the talk of kinship in war.

Shoulder to shoulder indeed. But when the dust settles, whose shoulders will sprout wings to escape, and whose will bear the weight of the rubble? Is there a bone, a tendon made for brotherhood—so forever we're joined as equals?

One journalist pushes past the others. "So will we see more combat helicopters on city tours, Colonel Lane? Will your so-called 'permanent-temporary presence' in Philippine territory be more permanent than temporary? How soon before we have stars and stripes flying in Manila's airspace?"

David Lane turns around, smiles broadly for the lens and emphatically denies any cause for anxiety. He wants to argue that U.S. forces are overstretched these days and have no intention of flying the flag over Philippine soil. But of course this will be refuted by "the American activity" in Mindanao, so he wishes everyone a Merry Christmas instead. "Season's greetings to you all. Rest assured we're working to the best of our ability for the good of both our homelands—and do call me David." He's not nicknamed "the people's colonel" for nothing. The tag always gives him heartburn. Heartburn is part of the job.

35

The broad smile fills the television. At 6.30 p.m. *City Flash* cleverly strings its news together. First, the meeting at Villamor Airbase, then a clip of a Philippine and U.S. joint military exercise, a few blank shots fired in the jungle, the death of an American hostage in Mindanao in 2002, then cut to the latest update on the shooting at the intersection. Pizza Hut has issued a statement that on the day of the shooting one of their motorcycles was stolen, so the assailant can't possibly be one of their men. The police must look elsewhere in their investigation, but the media is adamant about its best scoop yet.

Nena and Noland see their home again, the stretch of tracks and slums, the blinking stars, the traffic, and Eugene Costa's random interviews of Pizza Hut delivery boys looking wary and needing to get away. Then cut to Eugene interviewing Senator G.B. "Good Boy" Buracher at the wake of the murdered journalist.

When the reporter asks the senator what he thinks of the shooting, the bodyguards push the microphone aside, but G.B. chooses to answer. Any decent Christian would feel enraged by the salvaging and his heart bleeds for the bereaved family. The TV short-circuits; Noland hits it with his fist. It comes on again showing the widow of the victim screaming, "Murderer, murderer! How dare you come here, how dare you?" She's rushing at him while he's protesting his innocence, professing his deep sadness as his bodyguards bodily lift him out of the funeral parlor.

Nena grabs her son as if to suckle him. He can't breathe, but he wants to watch; he wants to see the face of the man accused of the murder, this "Good Boy" fallen from grace. He doesn't look like a Pizza Hut man. He rides in a tinted Pajero not a motorcycle, he wears a suit. But his mother turns off the TV. The hut grows dark. She rocks him, rocks herself soundlessly, trying to wish away the pain in her legs.

Outside the train is passing. It rocks both of them, even the woman sleeping on the mat. Soon he will return to his notebook of stories. He will add another comic strip, querying the cosmic.

A sky filled with stars.

Angel falling from the sky.

An empty sky.

He will hear his thoughts: *Whatever happened to his wings?*

36

Wings not clipped but resting in a bar. Bobby Cool likes it here. Never mind if it has gone down a grade or two. This hotel has been good to him for years. He likes its pouncing lion sign, now softened by mistletoe.

"So Mr. Bobby, are we settled about the lantern?"

He takes time to answer, slowly savoring his Johnnie Walker. He wants to gauge the thickness of the pocket of this very cultured voice. The Japanese speaks perfect English. He doesn't give his name or his room number, not yet.

"Difficult to order, sir, the lantern," he finally answers.

The other stares at his perfect fingers.

Bobby also gauges them by their hands. The more refined, the more generous. The more generous, the more discreet. The more discreet, the less hassle. He's hardly ever proven wrong. He likes this soft-spoken man who asks, "How can I make it easier for you, Mr. Bobby?" while the perfect fingers slip him three hundred dollars. A show of trust.

"I try, sir, I try."

"Yes, try please." The Japanese smiles politely.

"I take care of my lanterns, sir."

"I like the smaller one."

"But you don't know smaller one—"

"I've driven past, and I like it."

"Ah." Bobby pauses, tries another strategy. "Smaller one very new, sorry sir, and not shiny."

The perfect fingers add another three hundred. Then a faint sigh, as if he's suddenly tired. "Just pictures, Mr. Bobby, that's all I want."

37

It's eleven in the evening. There's a bigger crowd at the intersection, most of them nosing around. As Eugene Costa reported earlier, the crime scene has become a tourist attraction. Business is booming. The lantern, cigarette, and jasmine vendors, even the young carolers and beggars, have never been this busy. But not Bobby Cool. People are scrutinizing everything and everyone, so he can't maneuver his transactions. Everyone is on the case. Elvis and Noland can only sell lanterns now. Everyone is interested in lanterns. The journalist was probably shot after buying a lantern, there was one found in his car, and the American was probably choosing a lantern. Why else was she standing right here before she was shot, then abducted—but how do we know she's alive? And the Pizza Hut man drove from this point to that point for his getaway, possibly.

The traffic gets more clogged as the sleuthing goes on.

Vim, the lantern twin who was bashed, is noticeably absent, but his brother Vic is unfazed. Business is good, very good. Red, green, yellow, blue blink for only a little while before the star leaves the stall, headed back to some heaven. But the camera and film crews keep up the blinking lights. People offer themselves to be interviewed. Everyone has an opinion, a version of the Christmas crime and the Pizza Hut man mystery, and of course the missing American. It's a woman, a beautiful blond woman, they say.

Bobby watches his charges, intent on the smaller one. A weak debate goes on in his heart, under the gold cross that swings each time he moves. He's too young, but Elvis was even younger when he—and he's mute, his life's wretched, his mother's sick. All the more reason to rise to this occasion. In his own time, he did. Saved himself from the gutter—well, a nice man did. Clothed him, fed him, gave him a home, this gold cross, loved him. He was Australian. But he had to return to his country, so he passed him on to a friend. But he's able to live decently now. He has his own apartment, his stable business—with Elvis, a jackpot!

Noland gives Elvis five, and the other responds, giggling. "Now one more five—that's it, you're learning fast."

Noland smiles, one of those rare events.

"Smile more, man, it's Christmas!"

Bobby's phone rings. He takes the call, heads farther away from the crowd so he can hear, while calling out to the boys, "Stay put, both of you. Don't take off on me again, okay?"

38

Noland and Elvis sneak away, selling lanterns. All stars must go! There's perfect business with the cars and passers-by, and heaps of "Gimme fives" between the boys. Elvis attempts its rap version. He teaches Noland how to groove, man. "Okay to stray a bit from the boss," he whispers, turning his cap in full cocky revolution.

Noland protests against the venture—we'll get into trouble, we're out of our territory, we'll get bashed! But Elvis is cool about it. "Trust me, man, I know a route with no competition, and we'll pretend we're just picking up garbage, you know, with your cart." He winks.

They push across the highway, zigzagging through the traffic, making cars honk. Elvis yells at them, "Buy the best homemade star in the world!" or "Hoy, you trying to run us over?" He sneers at the street kids begging from cars, caroling from window to window. "Remember, Noland, begging is the worst, no dignity. I work, you work, so we deserve a reward. C'mon, man."

Noland gestures in protest, worried about Bobby Cool. He parks the cart against a lamppost, refusing to budge.

"Didn't I take you to the mall and you loved it?"

Yes, the lights, the lights. Noland closes his eyes. The lamplight catches his dreaming face.

"Hoy, wake up!" Elvis slaps his back and Noland grunts in protest. "Well, don't you want a bigger expedition? This one's unforgettable, man."

Noland waves his hands in the air, full of arguments.

Elvis gestures back, pretending he's mute, speaking in sign language even with his feet in the air. Then he's dancing—rap, dude, rap. Noland giggles. "Good, let's go then." Elvis pushes the cart along, past a store, an apartment, a garage of jeepneys, a warehouse, then another slum. He stops the cart, surveys the tinseled shanties, the winking lights.

"Wow, look at that...when all stars are lit, we can't feel poor...as if we've never been poor...."

The boys listen to the murmur of children still at play—hard to sleep three days before Christmas. The voices lean against each other, lift each other, like the scavenged wood, plastic, and cardboard keeping each other from tumbling down, keeping a home.

"Merry Christmas!" Elvis is bursting with insouciance. He throws up his cap and expertly catches it with his head. He shakes his arms and hips. "Bom-tarat-tarat—tararat-tararat-bom-bom-bom!" It's the catch-cry from the TV show *Wowowee*. Pitched toward the poorest, the show promises cash, a car, even a house. "Cash or basket?" Hope is dangled before the most desperate.

"Bom-tarat-tarat," Elvis yells out again.

"Tararat-tararat-bom-bom-bom!" The chant is picked up in the slums. A window opens and two kids do the trademark hip wiggle.

"See that, Noland? Everyone wants a piece of the action—bom-bom-bom!" he echoes the chant, the hip wiggle of hope that will later inspire a stampede of more than twenty-five thousand vying for a change of luck on a TV show. Seventy-four will be killed, one of them a four-year-old. How is it that hope grows too fully too soon, even before a full set of teeth?

"C'mon, Noland, I'll show you *real* action."

They stride on, stopping cars to sell lanterns. It's close to midnight but the jeepneys are still awake, missing each other by a hair's breadth. These are a legacy of forty years of American occupation, but made truly Pinoy. The American jeep was stripped of its grim army demeanor, then painted and polished to a tropical shine. Colorful banners and metal horses and the image of the Child Jesus, if not Mother Mary, were added, and behold—the Philippine jeepney was born. Passengers are skin to skin and eye to eye on two benches facing each other. With overpopulation, the city can't help but be hopelessly intimate. "Hoy, boys, give me a star," a driver calls out. The transaction is quick; the belching tail of the jeepney disappears in no time.

"Gimme a star, gimme five." Elvis slaps his friend's hand. "You know where we're going, man?"

Noland shakes his head.

"Of course I'm not telling, it's a surprise—bigger than the mall, man."

They cross another intersection where on school days jeepneys race with luxury cars. In this avenue of the richest university, kids get chauffeured to school, sometimes with their maid. Chauffeur and maid wait until their charges finish classes for the day.

"You'll love this place, Noland. One more intersection and we're there."

The cart rattles across the street close to what used to be Manila's busiest red-light district, until a zealous mayor closed the girlie bars and business went underground elsewhere. Farther up is one of the city's first shopping malls, which soon became a pick-up area. Foreign men with local girls or sometimes children in tow used to be as commonplace as merchandise. Shoppers would look the other way—too hard to think about it. The boys are close now. They're about to cross Roxas Boulevard, but Elvis pauses as a fish-ball vendor catches his eye. "Want a snack, Noland?"

Noland slaps his full pockets, does the little hip wiggle.

Elvis laughs; he can't believe what he's just seen. "That's what I mean, some *libog*, some sexy oomph, man," and he does his own wiggle. "Bom-bom-bom—so how many can you eat?"

They pig out. The vendor can't believe his luck. Elvis clowns about, singing the twelve days of Christmas, one line-one day before gobbling one stick of fish-ball that "my true love gave to me." Noland eats with him through twelve sticks, then drops giggling on the pavement, a mock-collapse. He wears his satiation like an old shirt.

39

Long ago, before electric lights, the very first lantern guided the faithful on their way to the pre-dawn mass, a nine-day tradition culminating in the Christmas Eve service. The first five-pointed star was made of bamboo strips wrapped in Japanese paper and lit with a candle. Delicately simple, it was a star guiding the feet to *the first star*.

And the Child was revealed. So was hope.

The resonances are startling. Over and over again, the same route, the same road signs. Perhaps the first star up there, the star in the hand and the star at the window are the very same hope lighting up the ribcage. "Almost there, Noland—look!"

High in the sky is a lit pinnacle, actually the hat of Santa Claus or some other magical creature at the entrance of a blazing complex.

"What do you think?"

Even the talk in Noland's head is silenced. He feels so tiny looking up at this giant mascot.

"It's the Star City, Noland."

A city inhabited by stars—is this possible?

"It has everything, all the rides of your dreams."

Have they come down from heaven, all of them?

Elvis has never seen his friend's face this awed, and afraid perhaps. This and the way Noland hugs himself makes his chest a little tight; he doesn't like the feeling. He tries to explain, "It's where you have Ferris wheels, bumper cars, roller coasters, Little Mermaid, Snow White, Horror House—" Then he stops. He sees nothing but incomprehension. "C'mon then, we'll go in," he says, taking Noland by the hand.

Noland doesn't budge.

"It's fun. C'mon, you'll love it."

Around them cars and taxis are ferrying children and

more children with their parents, aunties, uncles—the whole clan!

Children's heaven, no less. Noland allows himself to be led.

At the door, the guard stops them. He notes the shabby cart, thinks *street kids*. "Hoy, not allowed." He blocks the entrance.

Elvis can't believe his ears. He threatens to push the cart forward. "I have money, I can pay!"

The guard pushes the cart back. "Cart not allowed."

"I'll pay for it too—how much do you want?" He takes out a wad of pesos from his pocket.

Behind them the line of parents and nannies with their charges are getting impatient, complaining about being held up. A few are curious about how the altercation will pan out. There's brief cheering for the boys. "Aw, let them in, it's Christmas."

But the guard can't be seen to go back on his word. "You don't pay to me, you pay there." He motions to the counter inside. "But they won't let you in, so go away. You're holding up the line."

"Just because you have a gun!" Elvis spits out his contempt. "You think your cock is bigger!"

"You see," the guard shrugs his shoulders at the boys' supporters. Street kids running true to form, he almost adds, but can't be bothered.

"Come, Noland, we won't argue with that motherfucker." Elvis stomps off with the cart. He's fuming and his chest feels even tighter—no, it's on fire.

40

The Star City stands on a vast reclaimed area first developed under the Marcos dictatorship, when, as a journalist remarked, the first lady waved her hand and said, "Let there be land," and there was land. On it grew an imposing building devoted to the arts. Close by, an international convention center also sprang up a stone's throw from a five-star hotel. Some years later the largest shopping center in Asia will follow. How absurd that poverty exists where even the sea can be made solid with the flick of a hand.

There are lights everywhere, even out at sea. The Jumbo Floating Restaurant is like tinsel on water, meters away from the rich toys moored at the Manila Yacht Club. The boys stare at the Jumbo, resting for a while from their furious, silent stroll.

"People eat there, you know," Elvis snaps at no one.

Noland suspects the anger is aimed at him. It was his cart's fault they couldn't get in. He wants to make it up to his friend. He wants to tell him about the angel in the hut, that she's awake, that she's grown wings, that he fed her — no, he can't tell him that, he can't tell him anything now. His mother said not to say anything to anyone. Not about *her*. As if he can speak, as if he can even be understood.

"I hate you," Elvis snaps at the revelers ambling by. They scurry away from the crazy street kid who begins to rap and dance: "I hate you-motherfucker-you-motherfucker-you-you-you!"

Noland retreats, alarmed. His friend has the devil in him. He has a sneaking feeling that his mother is right, Elvis is the devil boy.

"C'mon, Noland, what's with you? You've never seen good rap, man?" he screams.

"Shut up!" someone screams back. It's a vagrant sleeping behind some bushes. "And wash your mouth out!"

Elvis rushes to the voice, Noland at his heels. "You wanna fight me, you wanna fight me-me-me?"

It's an old man curled on a plastic bag. He's on his feet in no time, rushing away, muttering, "Your mother should whip you, boy, whip you till that rotten mouth bleeds."

41

Nena can't sleep. She's folding laundry, her hands racing with her thoughts. Where's that boy? Where's that devil dragged him to this time? What's he up to? On TV the latest adolescent love duo sway like tinsel with their glittering costumes and earnest carol. Suddenly a news update cuts in. It's the police. Chief of Special Projects Roberto Espinosa is appealing to the public about the missing American, *Cate Burns*. She has a name now! Her photo is flashed on screen. Nena is transfixed. Espinosa says the American was last spotted at the scene of the shooting and possibly hurt too—maybe shot? A lantern seller and a taxi driver reported her "accidental involvement" in the Pizza Hut man mystery. She was just looking at those stars and then—the taxi driver returned her backpack too, such honesty, so fitting for this season. Let us emulate this Christmas spirit and help a guest of our country. The photo is flashed again.

Nena turns to the sleeping woman on the mat. *Dios ko*, she must go, she really must go.

The American consul comes on screen, reiterating the appeal from the Christmas party at the embassy. Colonel Lane is with her, wearing civilian clothes and his disarming smile. He wishes the Filipino people a Merry Christmas and invokes the long history of friendship between the two countries and how his grandfather fought the Japanese in the Second World War alongside brave Filipinos in the jungles of Bataan.... He falters slightly here, knowing that his wife is in the other room having Christmas cake with their two girls, that she has often accused him of trotting out his grandfather's history to get the sympathy vote, but it's my history too, for God's sake.

His wife fought him over Iraq; she took to the streets to protest. Home politics was bizarre, a heartbreak. Iraq shook their marriage, so he requested to be reassigned from the war zone and volunteered to make a difference in the Philippines. His grandfather loved this country with a fervor, its people, their quirky humor, their stoicism in war.... Colonel Lane turns on the smile again, saying he's here to follow in his grandfather's footsteps by assisting the joint military exercises under *Balikatan.* He stresses the value of friends "shouldering the load together"—so perhaps we can do this by helping a vulnerable American, a friend. He's rambling; too much champagne. He feels the usual heartburn coming on.

The lone journalist hovering in the background quizzes him, very casually. "David, we know the *Balikatan* is also designed to combat terrorism. Do you think this abduction could be a terrorist act against the United States? Lest you forget, we've had abductions before in Mindanao."

The consul neatly intervenes, emphasizing Philippine-American friendship, which has never failed, and reiterating that her government will be very grateful to whoever helps the lost American. She says her ambassador is currently at a meeting with Her Excellency the President of the Philippines, who is extremely supportive. She doesn't say it's a Christmas dinner at the palace where "the issue" is being diplomatically addressed.

Over canapés and champagne, a senator and a general secretly brainstorm the case. Who's assigned to it? Special Projects? Are they with us? Can't trust them, they love journalists over there, they could get "too involved." You should mobilize your own operations, General. It's worse than we think. No, I don't mean that "salvaged" journalist, I mean the American girl. The Burns family is well connected and you know there's pressure brewing, but we'll keep this under wraps. The ultimate solution lies with the intersection. It's been an ongoing problem—even the mayor complains about it. Those shanties have clogged the city drain forever, so the neighboring streets flood when it rains. It's a serious health hazard. And the criminal elements that breed in such congestion, one can't even begin to think—it's not just about the city, General, this is national security. Who knows, the Abu Sayyaf has now infiltrated Manila. So we must neutralize the area, let it breathe. Clean it up and relocate those poor things somewhere healthier and safer.

There are many politic ways to approach demolition. There are many ways to kill a cat.

Across the road from the embassy, Eugene Costa hints at a possible reward for any information on Cate Burns. He can't come closer. A truckload of soldiers barricading the gate watch his every move.

Nena turns off the television and crawls to the mat. She has a name now. *Cate Burns.* She watches the American sleep, then wonders whether she should hang the curtain again to hide her. She checks that the door is firmly shut. She's still afraid but the thought of a reward almost lightens her spirit.

42

Across the tracks, Helen is watching the broadcast on the reward, while Mario collects money from the short line of film viewers. Tonight it's a local action flick. He yells at his wife to turn on the video. He has to compete with firecrackers and carols from all directions.

"Hoy, can't you wait? I'm watching the news," Helen protests.

"News, news—how can there be news at this late hour?"

"And we don't have video sessions at this late hour."

"What can I do? People want to watch, Helen."

"People" is only Mikmik and her gang who have been pestering Mario that they really, really want to watch this film and they'd even pay double.

"Double's not enough, there's only four of you. I'll lose out—electricity's so expensive these days. That wire-man's a pain, as you know."

Mikmik begins to cry.

"What now?" Mario asks, scratching his head.

"I just want some relief, Mang Mario, my mother has forgotten me. She didn't send anything this Christmas. For the first time she didn't even send a Christmas card. Ay poor me, poor me." She winks at the other girls behind her. They've made a bet: she insists she'll pull this off beautifully. The man's a muffin-heart, a softie, a regular sucker—you'll lose your twenty pesos to me, girls. Watch this—"Mang Mario, imagine if you had children of your own and you went abroad, do you think you'd forget them?" and she starts sniffling again.

It's a sore point for Mario and Helen, the fact that they can't have kids. "Ay, Mikmik, it's very late ... but okay, okay, girl—hoy, Helen, I said we'll have a last full show."

As she puts on the action flick, Helen keeps hearing Eugene Costa's voice: a reward, a reward, a reward.

43

Across the city, another woman is watching the news in a bed strewn with papers. She's organizing a public campaign against her husband's murderer. "Who is the Pizza Hut man?" When she heard it on TV for the first time, she started laughing, each laughing breath pushed out of her lungs in haste, as if she'd die if it weren't all laughed out, and quickly. She found herself on the floor, laughing and tearing at her hair.

Lydia de Vera hasn't slept since then. Tonight the papers are a comfort. She finds her husband's old files on every corrupt official in the country, and his newspaper articles that grew bolder through the years. Why did you have to be so brave? And you had to be stupid to be brave—funny, that. But it doesn't make her laugh.

They'd been married for only two years. They did university together; he, journalism, and she, political science. "The young activist couple," "the radical couple," "the idealists," "the lefties": the newspapers made the most of the string of labels and their photos, depending on the writer's or the photographer's political intent, depending on whether they were friends of her husband or stooges of the senator. The small talk about her husband was as varied. He was the enemy. He was a fool. He was a hero. To her, he is Germinio, her lost Jimmy.

DECEMBER 22

44

It's after midnight and the newspaper trucks are already on the road, ferrying the new headlines. Cate Burns's photo has usurped Germinio de Vera's. The lost American is the new face of the Pizza Hut man mystery. Things have moved on quickly, even at a late-night market where the boys are sitting down for a feeling-better snack.

Elvis has simmered down. "Food cures everything," he says, then a sip of noodle soup, a gulp of Coke, a long sigh. "Thank God for Coke, all that fish-ball is now going down smoothly.... I was sort of clogged a while ago." He offers a reason for his rage. "Would you like some barbecue?"

Noland doesn't respond. He sits slightly apart. He thinks of the old man stumbling away in fear.

"Well, I'm having one—with chili sauce." Elvis orders.

"Sorry boy, I've run out," the stall vendor answers.

"See how lucky I am?" Elvis sighs into his noodles.

Noland notes the shoulder sag. He hasn't turned his cap at all, not since Star City.

"I'm no street kid, I work," he mutters between slurps.

Noland sidles back to his friend, slurps along.

At the other end of the market, Eugene Costa is also eating his noodles. His shift is done and tomorrow is another big assignment. Ah, Senator G.B. will hate him, but it's more than worth it. He remembers how at the wake the widow led an old woman to the open coffin. She stood there staring, then tugged at the widow's sleeve, pointing to the bunch of little white roses on the dead man's chest. At first the widow couldn't understand what her mother-in-law meant, but when she did, she plucked a rose and handed it to her. The old woman held it to her nose and smiled, whispering, "*Pitimini,*" and allowed herself to be led away. She identified the rose but not her son, perhaps not even death. Then the senator arrived with his bodyguards and the widow started screaming, going for him. The old woman stood in the middle of the room, rose in hand, looking on curiously.

The memory makes Eugene feel tired to his bones. He'll sleep a bit, if he can. He'll be back around this boulevard early tomorrow—but it's tomorrow now. Maybe he shouldn't crash, just have a stroll, get some sea into his lungs; the city won't sleep anyway. He misses the sea in the province, but he can't go home this

Christmas. Work. He must call his mother. She'll be disappointed, but he'll make it at New Year.

He'll sleep a bit, if he can.... That man in the coffin ... it could be him, it could be anyone in this business of telling the truth.

45

"What happened to your mouth—I mean, why don't you speak?"

Noland opens his mouth wide, close to the other's face.

Elvis clowns, "Ugggh, bad breath."

They laugh. Friends again.

They're at the other side of Roxas Boulevard now, at a park with a fountain amid giant lanterns, not just star ones but flower and fruit ones, and no one is sleeping. The park is crowded with revelers. Elvis catches two girls, aged about five and six and feral looking, trying to clamber up the cart. Their mat is spread under the tree behind the parked cars.

"Hoy, leave that alone," he warns. "It's ours."

The girls giggle and get into the cart anyway.

"Such cheek. Well, okay, just for a while, and don't hurt it."

The boys sit by the fountain, mixing with the Christmas crowd, one eye on their cart. "Feels right,

THE SOLEMN LANTERN MAKER   117

don't you think? We're like everybody," Elvis murmurs and fastidiously turns his cap this way and that.

Local carols blast from an open car. Elvis sings along, then suddenly remembers. "So, she awake yet?"

Noland shrugs; he can't tell.

"If she never wakes, you're in deep shit. What if she sleeps forever in your house?"

Noland skips a heartbeat. "Forever in your house." It's all he hears.

"Yoohoo, hello Noland, knock-knock, you there? Hard to tell what goes on in there."

An hour later a girl about Elvis's age strides to the cart. She has a baby on her hip and is about to lay it beside the other girls.

"Ooops, hold it, that's ours!" Elvis rushes forward.

"Yours? They're my sisters," the girl protests.

"Okay, out!" Elvis orders the two girls in the cart, but they won't budge.

"See, it's *ours*!" The bigger girl stamps her foot, triumphant.

"Okay, then," Elvis says and begins to push the cart away, Noland behind him. The two girls scramble out while big sister hurls curses at him. Elvis turns around and comes very close to her. "I don't normally hit girls."

The other backs off, still cursing.

"Hmph, street kids," Elvis grunts. "They're dangerous— we're not having any luck, are we? Maybe we should buy ourselves guns, Christmas guns. What do you think, Noland?"

A man with toy revolvers slung around his neck has just wandered past.

Noland pulls at his friend's arm. Let's leave, let's cross the street. He can still hear the girl murmuring curses under her breath as she settles down with the others on the mat.

46

Two more hours and it will be the early Christmas mass. Elvis plonks himself at the church door. "Finally, peace, but of course...." He raises his arms to make a point about their location. They're just across the park, but how quiet here by contrast, except for two security guards pacing the nearly empty car park, arguing about whether the Pizza Hut man is a *real* terrorist. They get distracted when the boys arrive. Look, one's pulling out wads of pesos from his pocket. Ah, you never know what characters come here.

"So, Noland, let's divvy up the lantern loot. Now that's the loot, and this is my own money from before." Elvis spreads out the cash.

Noland empties his pockets too. He wonders where Elvis gets his money, lots of it, and he never runs out.

"Jackpot!" Elvis claps his hands. "Now how much do we declare to the boss?" He winks at Noland. "Here, you get most of the loot—it's your lanterns, remember—

and when Bobby asks you, say business was so-so." He makes the empty palm not-so-good gesture, and giggles.

Noland echoes the little act. He's content. My friend is a good devil boy. He looks up. The few trees are hung with stars, simple ones, just five points plainly lit. He looks farther up, but he can't see the others. He can't make out the real ones.

47

The guards are worried. Should we follow those boys inside?

Those boys are just exploring; at least Noland is. He notes there are only white stars hanging in a row up there. Again five simple points and plainly lit. This is a good church. He remembers the many colors in Quiapo, too many. But what does he know about good churches? Aside from one or two visits when they were new in Manila, and lately the little side-trip in Quiapo, he remembers nothing. Not how his parents used to take him as a baby to mass. Or how he was baptized with the perfect name at his father's request. He hears Elvis laughing at the entrance, beside himself with mirth over a sign at the window.

Attention:
To our dear parishioners.

> *Please do not leave your*
> *Personal belongings unattended.*
> *Somebody might think they're the*
> *"Answer" to their prayers.*

He strides up to his friend. "Oh Noland, Noland, you should see this, this is so funny, so clever—"and he sits down on the front pew, giggling. The one good thing about his pimp was that he taught him English, and he was a smart student, but not in speaking. Anyway it's good for business to know the language, even if it's only in your head and not in your tongue, more so because business should be foreign. There's not much going with the measly peso. "You should read it, man. C'mon."

Noland sees only black squiggles on white. Besides, something else has caught his eye. On the left side of the altar is the nativity with the lifelike Joseph and Mary looking down on tiny Jesus. Mother and father look with full attention at their child; the child looks with full attention at Noland.

"Hoy, Noland, do you ever wonder why they're all white, even all saints, all angels are white? Because heaven is white and God's Amerkano."

Noland's not listening. He touches Mary's cheek, Joseph's beard.

Elvis slaps Jesus's palm. "Gimme five, white boy!"

"Hoy—hoy!" It's one of the guards striding in. He has to assure himself, ease the worry. "Just what're you doing, huh?"

"What do you think—stealing Jesus?"

The guard stammers, closes his mouth again.

Elvis starts laughing, pointing at the warning sign. "I might think he's the 'answer to my prayers'—ha-ha-ha!"

"Have you no respect?"

"I'm paying my respects."

Again the guard loses his tongue. Elvis is enjoying himself. He's getting his own back at all the guards in the world.

Noland leads him away, fearful he'll lose it again as he did in Star City.

"Don't worry, I'm not staying, sir. I don't do mass, so bye-bye."

Still the guard can't drag anything from his mouth.

48

Outside the guards argue. One wants to throw the children out; the other says it's unchristian. Anyway the children are out in the car park, which is now slowly filling up. The guards agree not to make a scene, but they watch the children's every move. They're pushing the cart around and around, Elvis protesting, "No, I don't do mass."

Noland tugs at Elvis's sleeve. How to explain that he wants to stay, not for the mass but for those three inside. Mother, father, child. He wants to look at them again.

"I used to, mass I mean."

Noland stops the cart. It's the first time Elvis has spoken of his past. He waits for more.

Elvis lights a cigarette, offers to share with Noland, who shakes his head. "See that?" They have stopped before the Crucifixion in gray plaster, or is it marble, half lit in a little garden. "That's Jesus, the big Jesus. With his mother and those two other women." He takes in a lungful. "Gory stuff...pain, suffering." He turns away, hides his face.

It's an awkward moment. Noland looks away too.

"You like those three inside. Oh, they're okay...but fancy being born in a stable...don't know where I was born...don't know who birthed me...don't wanna know—and you, you wanna know?"

Noland can't find the courage to nod his head.

Elvis stares at the glowing tip of his cigarette, letting it burn. "You think Jesus had a brother? Would have been nice...safe. His brother would have fought all those bad soldiers off...saved him from the cross or something."

Noland worries that his friend speaks strangely, his voice sounds as if he's very tired, as if he's not Elvis. And he doesn't want to look at big Jesus now, or Elvis, so he must look elsewhere too. Again he squints at the sky for the lights farther up, but it's impossible to see anything. It's too bright down here.

She looks up. The lanterns are lit in rainbow colors lulled by a soft breeze. The vision is spectacular. The hut is a wonderland of shining paper stars. They're too many, too difficult to count all. She uses her ten fingers, even her ten toes, then starts all over again with little success.

A boy is staring at her counting. She's embarrassed at her ineptness.

The breeze becomes a gust of wind, buffeting the stars around, but they're still hanging from the strings up there. She keeps counting.

The boy offers his ten fingers, his ten toes.

She got it wrong. It's not wind, it's something else, that sound. It's a motorcycle revving, whipping up wind.

The boy holds up both his hands, but not for counting. He's trying to tell her something. His mouth is open but no sound—everything has grown silent. It revs close, one lantern is shot, the paper bursts, the light shatters. Another lantern is shot, then another and another. The stars begin to bleed, the blood dropping on her. She wakes up screaming, "He shot him, he shot him!"

Nena holds her, cooing, "Okay-okay...shhh...shhh." After a while, the stars up there are whole again. Cate touches her head, her belly. Her face travels through time, crumples in grief. "I lost it...I lost—" She begins to sob. Nena holds her tighter. "No-cry, no-cry, Cate Burns."

"You know me?" Cate asks, suspicious now.

Nena is silent.

Suddenly Cate remembers, "My passport, my bag—" She remembers more. "The taxi...oh God, I have to go, I have to go to the embassy—"

"No-go, no-go!" Nena quickly crawls to the door, blocks it.

Cate stares, suddenly fearful. Who is this woman? Nena, yes, that's what she said—with a son named Noland. He took her here, she remembers a cart. Why are they keeping her here? Do they know about the shooting—maybe they—oh my God! "I've no money on me now, but I can pay you if I get my things from the embassy, or I can make a call, is there a phone around here, no, where can I find one, where is this place, oh no I have nothing on me, can you lend me some money, you can't keep me here, are you keeping me here, am I a hostage, oh God, are you in *this* too?"

Nena keeps shaking her head. She can't follow this rapid burst of English. She can only understand that this woman is terrified, of her. But I won't hurt you, Cate.

Cate steps toward her, trying to sound calm. "Where's your son? Maybe he can take me to a phone? Noland—he can—"

Nena shakes her head. "No Noland, no come home."

Cate persists. "Look, I'll pay if you let me go, I'll give you money—yes, money—" and she makes the sign for it, rubbing her fingers together.

Nena nods; maybe she's trying to tell her about the reward. Her face is inches from hers, she can smell her panic, no you can't go out there, not now, not in the light, they'll all know, and then, and then—Nena pushes her back with all her strength.

Cate falls. Nena crawls to her feet, hugging them to her breast, and like a suppliant begs, "No-go, please no-go."

Around the hut, the angels almost sigh.

51

They have stayed for the mass, much to the guards' greater worry. What if they make trouble now?

Before the Crucifixion, Elvis grew talkative, then taciturn. He took off his cap and squatted there, his back to the big Jesus. When the mass started, he didn't stay the hand that pulled him inside and sat him down.

Noland feels as if the warmth in his chest will spill over. He keeps checking the family in the stable, while trying not to miss every bit of the ceremony, every move of the white priest. How can he be white? Because Elvis is right, God's Amerkano. The priest is in fact Irish and well loved in the parish. He speaks fluent Pilipino. Noland can't believe it. *They speak my language in heaven!* The priest looks like someone's grandfather; he opens his arms like he's about to hold everyone. This feels right, this feels so familiar. Noland stands-sits-kneels with everyone, as if it were the most natural thing to do.

Outside the guards are checking the cart parked before the Crucifixion. One guard is convinced it's blocking the way so the other pushes it from the main thoroughfare. "There, satisfied?" he asks. "Worrying will do no good. We'll keep our eyes open and it'll be okay. We can't afford a scene."

When "Silent Night" comes on, the same guard whispers, "That always gets me, you know . . . sung like that."

The ancient Christmas carol is sung by a boy whose voice hasn't broken yet, an angel voice. Noland closes his eyes, letting the song wash over him, take him elsewhere. *I know a story you don't know.* He dreams up another comic strip. Perhaps it is prayer.

Empty sky.

Fallen angel on the ground.

Fallen angel ascending.

Sky with shining star.

52

Bobby is in a taxi, scouring the streets, cursing under his breath. It's 6 a.m. He hasn't slept. "Try Roxas Boulevard, the Baywalk," he tells the driver. "And go slow. We're looking for two boys with a cart."

The metro aides are busy sweeping up last night's revelry. A group of joggers zigzag through the clean-up. One remarks about the photo of Cate Burns on a newspaper. Some older folks are taking in the sea breeze, alongside stragglers from last night trying to clear their heads. Traffic is picking up. The lanterns at each lamppost are now simply plastic decorations, not the shining stars, flowers, or fruit of last night. Magic sleeps in the morning.

It's that Elvis, he should have never trusted him. He's crazy that boy, precious crazy. The clients adore his aplomb, he makes them laugh, he's very good, a goldmine for some years now, and he likes his job. He likes the fringe benefits, the food, the huge tips, the luxurious overnights, sometimes the out-of-town holidays. He laps them up. He likes to hang out by the sea in the early hours, so he could be anywhere now. "I said, slow down," Bobby scolds the driver. Elvis loves it here, often sitting with the cool men and daring his pimp to tell him he's not as cool.

Under the palms along Manila Bay, the statues do look cool. Mayor Arsenio Lacson sits on a park bench, reading the paper, and Senator Ninoy Aquino points to the horizon, hopeful before the tragic tarmac incident at the airport now named after him. His murder went through years of investigation that petered out into doubtful justice. Ninoy's gaze is fixed ahead, a visionary's attitude or perhaps he's just searching for two boys and a cart. Like the bronze President Ramon Magsaysay across the road, shielding his eyes from the sun to see better, perhaps looking for some speck in the horizon. *My country's children small as hope.*

Bobby's phone rings. He breathes in deeply and takes the call. Bobby pours his apology into his cupped palm. "Sorry, sir, very sorry, I promise but there's problem, only a little, I fix—yes, I promise, sir, and I keep my promise, but—yes, yes, I will, sir." Absentmindedly he unbuttons his shirt as he speaks. He needs to air his mea culpas for not getting the lantern delivered last night. "I promise. You get pictures today."

53

Locked in, the hut is a world of angels and two women. Nena and Cate are sizing up each other warily. The winged creatures are fascinated by this earthly wariness. Nena is still blocking the door, caught between anxiety and hope. Cate is sitting on the mat, between fear and grief. What an unlikely tableau, like a forced pause in a play, but the angels hear a conversation: two different tongues, two different intentions.

Cate: I can make a run for it.

Nena: *Ang reward... puwede kaming mag-Christmas.*

Cate: Surely she can't run after me...

Nena: *Baka makapag-aral si Noland...*

Cate: But where do I go?

Nena: *Nasaan ba ang batang 'yun?*

Cate: My chance... out that door and...

Nena: *Pero walang pulis, walang uniporme...*

How to cross the miles between them? A mother's hopes for her son, maybe a real Christmas or possibly an education, even till high school, which she never finished—if they get that reward. But no police, no uniforms, please. The other hopes for only one thing: escape. Maybe the angels speculate and wager among themselves. Let's see what they do, how they bridge this divide.

Nena tries. "You sleeping long time."

She gets no response.

"Noland watching you long time."

Still silent.

"He like you. You like dress? You like slippers?"

Cate turns around—okay, she'll play along. "I like him too. I'd like to thank him for these," she fondles her blue housedress, "so tell him to come. He can help me, he can take me to a phone—please?"

"Sorry, no Noland."

This is useless. She's been giving this same lie for an hour. Yes, she must be lying. Why doesn't she leave that fucking door?

"No Noland, no son, no son, no son—see?" Nena

waves her empty palms around to make the point. Why can't this woman understand that he hasn't come home?

Cate is silent, then like a late echo, "No son..." Her breath catches. It's the snag in the lungs, unmistakable to Nena. Maybe *it* was a boy. Instinctively she crawls forward, saying, "Sorry-sorry...baby...." but the other makes a move toward the door so Nena rushes back to it, blocking it apologetically.

"Okay-okay, Cate, me understanding," she pleads her case, massaging her knees under the housedress, trying to calm the little gnawing mice. "Baby die... mother sad-sad...father sad-sad."

She is desperate to commiserate, but Cate hears only one thing. She protests bitterly. "No sad father."

Nena looks perplexed, then nods. "No father? Ah, no husband...sorry for you...me understanding...me no husband."

The women are silent. Above them, the hanging lanterns are ghostly shadows. After a while, Nena asks, "Hungry?"

54

Hungry at 8 a.m., so McDonald's then. Elvis takes Noland to his favorite joint. Noland hesitates. "C'mon, brother," Elvis beckons, "they have fantastic breakfast here, my blowout."

They fall in line like everyone else—the office workers, the teenagers still groggy from last night, even a man in a business suit anxiously whispering on his cell phone about how his U.S. deal might crash because of this latest terrorist act, you know, the case of that Burns woman.

When it's their turn, Elvis nudges Noland—watch this, listen to this, nothing beats this, man.

"Your order, sir, is two pancakes and two hamburgers and two hot chocolates to have here, and two more pancakes and hamburgers to go, and you gave me five hundred pesos." The till rings, the hot food slides onto the tray.

Elvis isn't called "sir" anywhere else. McDonald's is the best joint.

Noland is worried and he doesn't understand English anyway. He keeps looking at the clock on the wall. His mother is surely furious by now. The big breakfast makes his stomach warm, though, and he's never had these flat things with sweet, sweet water on them. "Pancakes," Elvis explains. And the cart, he keeps checking the cart through the window. The guard said he'd watch over it; he has nothing against carts or children with carts. Noland didn't see Elvis slip him a fifty-peso note. His friend is his old self again, fussing over his cap.

Outside there are street kids begging and singing a carol with a tambourine made of Coke bottle caps. Elvis slips them a twenty on the way out. He feels perfect. Close to the water like this, he's on top of the world.

He'll sit with that mayor what's-his-name on the park bench, get his nose on his newspaper and watch Noland's eyes go wide, ahhh. He'll take him for a stroll under the palm trees, count the yachts with him, tell him the names of the big hotels, about their cool rooms, their big beds, let him know he's lived the good life, yeah—

He barely gets a word out when a hand grabs him by the nape and drags him into a taxi. It's Bobby pinning him down, growling at him. "I knew I'd find you here. You have the nerve to run out on me, you little shit! Now let's do *real* work—and you too, Noland, get in!"

Outside the street kids watch with interest. Noland protests, motioning toward his cart and holding up the bag of breakfast that he's taking home. He's sorry he ran away, he'll make up with more lanterns tonight. His hands weave deep apologies in the air.

Elvis pleads, "Bobby, I'm game, but not Noland, he's not in this, he has no clue, not him, Bobby, not him, I'm game, I'll do all jobs, I'll make up for last night, I'll do double jobs, I promise, but not Noland."

Bobby drags Noland in; there's a struggle. The McDonald's bag falls, breakfast scatters on the pavement. As the taxi speeds away, the street kids rescue breakfast. The littlest one jumps into the cart and the others push it away. They leave, eating and singing "Jingle Bells."

55

The helicopter is back. Again it hovers low over the famous intersection. Again the strip looks up, anxiously. They've seen that Cate Burns on TV so many times in the last twenty-four hours. Even Mikmik and her gang are without their old bravado now, wishing the lost Amerkana would be found so there won't be any of the wars that Mario's boasting about. He's seen them all on video, oh yes! And if she's found, there'll be a reward . . . yes, what about that reward?

Inside the hut Cate and Nena are also looking up, their faces lit by the sun streaming through the cherub's face. Outside it's a blazing midday.

Cate is hopeful. It's a helicopter flying very low, the second time now. What if . . . Nena is scared; those flying things make her think of locusts.

Dark and light: a closed hut and the sun insistently creeping in. The stars strung from the roof are lit. For want of something to say Nena points to them, whispering, "Star . . . *parol . . . parol.*"

"*Parol. . . .*" Cate instinctively echoes.

Nena nods. "Noland make . . . ay, Noland," then strikes her breast. Her son has never been this late, but there's room for hope. On the floor are the remains of bread and Milo. The women have eaten together.

At the public pump, the bond is alien to hope. Helen, Manang Betya, Lisa and the other women are finishing their laundry over whispers suddenly hushed by the helicopter. *Dios ko*, it's back in the air. That thing is the ultimate proof, you better believe it. Why do you think traffic's been rerouted from this intersection? And did you see the truckload of soldiers in the next street? And the bulldozer? When that thing lands, it's over.

The women can't hear themselves with the Huey whipping the air, thumping at their ribcage, usurping this habitation. Hands panic with the washing. Beat, rinse, wring, beat, rinse, wring. And flush down the city drain. This is what they'll do to us. It happens. They'll clean us up.

"It's because of that Amerkana, you know—"

"Why, is she God that she can move heaven and earth?"

"And uproot our lives?"

"I refuse to listen to gossip." Helen rises, shaking. Fear with fury is enough to make one brave. She shoulders her laundry paddle and walks off. Yesterday she had thought of that Amerkana with hope, what with the talk about a reward, and now it's punishment. Indeed, is she God?

"Hoy, Helen, what's with you?" Lisa is on her feet too.

"I'm going to ask—I've the right to know, don't I? This is *my* home!"

"You want to get into trouble?"

"You want to get shot?"

But the other women soon march with her to the next street. Might as well know. The troop of housedresses, two with babies, pick up others along the way, even Mikmik's gang.

In the next street, they crowd the bulldozer and Helen thumps it with her laundry paddle. The driver's attention is caught. He looks down the immense steel barrel. The others hold their breaths.

"Hoy, is it true?" Helen calls out, hands planted on her hips.

The driver is perplexed. "What—what's true?"

"That you'll clean up the intersection?" Manang Betya finds her voice, her fingers fondling both rosary and *jueteng* notebook in her pocket.

"And at Christmas too?" Mikmik pushes her way forward, blowing her trumpet at the man. "How dare you?"

"Don't know what you're talking about." The driver scratches his head, caught off guard by the assault. "Ask them over there." He motions to the truckload of soldiers a few meters away. "I'm just a paid hand."

Mikmik and her gang blow their trumpets up at him and the other women jeer. "Paid hand, hah!"

In an instant the woman with the baby clambers up onto the bulldozer and hands him the child.

"Wha—?"

"Take him, take him too, if you take away the roof over his head."

The other women are stunned. Then slowly they begin to applaud, as the driver stammers through his response and quickly hands the baby back. Meanwhile three uniforms have moved forward from the truck, rifles slung over their shoulders. When they reach the bold group, the applause dies. Silence and furtive glances at the rifles.

"What's this, aunties?" one of the soldiers asks in a deferential tone. No one speaks. "I'm asking."

"Is—is it true?" Manang Betya whispers. "The demolition?"

He chuckles, shakes his head. "Who's been gossiping, huh?" He surveys the ragtag of housedresses, mostly wet. "Go home and finish your washing," he cajoles, pushing them back playfully with his rifle, but when the other men frown, he lets the weapon slide back on its strap. "Go home. What demolition? You've been watching too much TV drama. Go, go."

The women eye the rifles, hesitate, then shuffle back home. None is able to make a sound, despite the howl in each throat. But such is terror, it's always lonely. The knotting of the body is yours alone.

Back at the public pump, it's beat, rinse, wring once again, and a faint whisper, "It's because of that Cate...."

The helicopter is now following the traffic at Roxas Boulevard where everyone is looking up. Look, those stars and stripes threaten this season's peace and goodwill, but oh that poor lost Cate, who's now spoken of on a first-name basis after so much drumming up by the media, and oh that Pizza Hut terrorist man whose identity has expanded with terrified speculations....

Everyone is looking up. Everyone is missing the two boys with a pimp in a taxi, down here at ground level.

"Shut up! It's better to be good boys rather than poor boys, you hear?"

"*Putang ina mo*—your mother's a whore, Bobby!" Elvis screams.

"Watch your mouth!"

Elvis keeps arguing with the pimp, but Noland has flown away. His eyes are shut. He's listening for his angels, but there's only the drone of the helicopter. He shuts his eyes tighter.

The comic strip is empty. It's just a strip of boxes now.

56

The venue has changed but Bobby isn't surprised. No longer that bar with the pouncing lion sign, and it's five stars this time. The hotel lobby is tastefully decked. Christmas glitter that's not too loud, mostly traditional designs; the shell lantern is the main motif. Bobby is convinced. The man has class and is extremely discreet. The text message was brief, no names, just the new hotel and room number for Mr. Bobby.

The boys are wearing fresh clothes, and carry lanterns in their hands. The pimp has been extra careful to achieve the right look. He orders coffee for himself,

Coke for the boys. He makes small talk for the ears of an English family close by who are waiting for the airport shuttle, the father reading the papers, the mother bouncing her baby. Sometimes she smiles at the two boys and their lanterns. "Look, sweetie, stars!" she coos to her daughter.

Bobby smiles back and keeps up his small talk, dropping in English words here and there. "*Miss n'yo si dad, di ba*—you missed your dad, right? Of course, after five long years abroad." He buttons up Noland's shirt, pats Elvis's head. Elvis growls.

"Don't push it, Elvis," he whispers, then to Noland adds more audibly, "It's not polite to stare." He smiles apologetically at the woman and her baby.

Noland is staring at a familiar face on the back of the husband's newspaper, nudging Elvis secretly. Look, look it's *her*!

Elvis tries to make out the caption, then nudges him back. *Cate Burns.* That's her name. And they say she's been shot and kidnapped! Elvis takes Noland's hand, presses it hard. I told you it was crazy to take her home, crazy-crazy—what if?

Noland returns the pressure and shifts uneasily on the deep sofa, the stars slipping from his lap. *The whole world knows.*

57

Noland is still not home. The women are sitting closer on the floor, a candle between them. Cate has stopped wondering if she can make a run for it. Earlier Nena pleaded with her and somehow something came through the fog. *The boy has not come home,* simple as that, but it's tearing apart this mother's heart. She can see it now, it's no lie, it makes her less doubtful, especially when Nena says, "Okay you go...tomorrow...but wait Noland please-please, okay?" She's clasping her legs to her chest, her face contorted.

"You okay, Nena? Your legs—?"

The other woman turns away, mumbling, "Accident...."

"Can I do anything?"

"No!"

Cate shrinks from the violent response, as if the woman has just spat at her.

From her window, Helen is looking at the silent hut across the tracks. She can't clear the cobwebs in her head. I wonder if Nena knows about that bulldozer. It's still there, waiting—ay, what if we lose our homes? And what's happened to those two? It's been silent in there since yesterday, no sign of mother and son. I hope they're okay, what with these murders and now a demolition, *Dios ko* ... I wonder when that helicopter will land, when that bulldozer will start moving... I wonder where that Cate is... I think they suspect we've all kidnapped her.

Helen is sorting videos and laundry, nearly folding in a video with the laundry—ay, stupid me! Then she pauses, slips into a dream, wondering how much is the reward. For a devout Catholic, it's easy to mix up the carrot and the stick. Heaven and hell. Paradise and brimstone. It's easy to be torn apart.

She leaves her chore, studies the hut across, listens for any sound—nothing. Noland didn't fetch water at the pump today...that's strange. There's something about that hut, she feels it in her chest. She finally walks across and knocks at the door. "Hoy, Nena, Noland, you there? You okay?"

Inside Nena freezes. Cate walks to the door, about to open it. Helen calls out again. Nena blows out the candle.

Helen walks around the hut, trying to peek in. She's almost sure she saw some light inside, some movement. She knocks the third time. "Nena, Noland!"

Nena crouches lower on the floor, making herself small.

Cate peers through the crack bisecting the angel at the door. The neighbor is walking away. She almost calls her back, but hesitates. She turns toward Nena; she can't see a thing now. She gropes her way back, almost tripping over the terrified woman on the floor. She sits down again.

When all is silent, Nena whispers, "Thank you."

Cate makes a little sympathetic sound, to fill the darkness, and the other does the same. "My son...he good hands...he make star many-many...he make story many-many...." Nena whispers, pausing here and there to make sure her guest is still listening, or perhaps her heart. Listen, listen.

There is room for hope. I know a story you don't know, that you can know.

58

A camera clicks, light flashes. Noland's closed eyes. Another click, another flash. Noland's mouth in repose. Noland's full head. Noland's torso. Noland's feet. Noland's whole body sleeping in the middle of a king-size bed. He's wearing a pink silk kimono. At his feet is a geisha doll, also in silk. On the bedside table is a Christmas toy, a drummer boy. Tinsel is draped on it, just a hint of glitter, quite tasteful. Farther away, on a large table, is food just as tasteful: grapes, cheese and biscuits, two bottles of fine red, a Christmas ham, a box of Belgian chocolates, all partly feasted on. The used plates and cutlery and wine glasses are neatly stacked. Two people had a quiet party.

The camera clicks again, the light flashes: Noland's face waking up.

"Good evening, boy. Ah, long sleep." Soft voice, impeccable English, barely a Japanese accent. "Hungry maybe?"

Noland slowly gets up, tries to remember where he is. His head is heavy, his tongue thick, his eyes can't focus yet. He's wearing a dress he thinks, with nothing underneath. He pulls it around him, tighter. He stares at the Japanese with his camera. He's also wearing a dress?

"That's a nice face." The camera clicks. "You like the toys?"

Noland understands the nod toward the toys as a go-ahead. He picks up the geisha. Why's her face so white? Is she meant to be dead? He drops her quickly, then picks up the drummer boy. He turns it around and around. Each action is shot by the camera.

"That's for you." The man comes closer, winds up the drummer boy with his perfect hands. It starts drumming. "Like it?" He pats Noland on the head like a proper father or uncle.

Noland picks it up and it drums in mid-air.

A shot of Noland with the toy.

"Ah, beautiful boy...now, take it off, please...." The perfect fingers tug at his own kimono to make the point.

59

In the suite next door, the scene is less proper, less pretty. The clothes and bedcovers are strewn all over the floor, empty beer bottles and half-eaten burgers and chips sit on travel brochures, and the television is on, loud. It is *City Flash* on the famous crime, with the voice-over of the taxi driver wondering whether the American was actually abducted by street kids, because she was sort of *with them* when it happened. More witnesses from the intersection have also come forward to tell their version of the incident; in fact there are many versions now. And yes, there were street kids, yes, she was talking to them, yes, we'll do anything to help find her. No, we had nothing to do with her kidnapping.

There are louder voices from the shower.

The news continues. The taxi driver is under police protection—and is possibly being interviewed by U.S. officials? There's protest against America meddling with Philippine affairs, besides this is a civilian matter, or are we seeing the usual neo-colonialism? Human rights activists are enraged over the rumor that the military have ordered the demolition of the intersection, but the Chief of Special Projects, Roberto Espinosa, dispels all anxiety. The police, the military, and Philippine and American agencies are collaborating to solve this crime, which is made even more shocking by the fact that it was committed in a season of peace and goodwill.

In the shower, a man's voice negotiates. "But I paid the full price!"

"No, don't like," Elvis snaps back.

"You'll like, I'm gentle," the man cajoles, then sneers. "Don't tell me you're a virgin?"

The Philippine president commiserates with the

American ambassador, emphasizing the friendship between the two countries. She invokes their joint military exercises for an urgent cause: the war against terrorism. The anchorwoman asks, "Is this abduction a terrorist act?"

"Just suck, that's deal, okay?" Bobby said.

"You and your pimp want to rip me off? C'mon, don't make me wait, boy. Turn around, I said turn around, you cheat!"

The shower is steamed up, as if there's a fog. Behind the glass, two bodies struggle. A boy is screaming, "Fuck you, fuck you!" his body flattened on the glass, his hands held up, as the man grunts, "Yes, I'm fucking you, I'm fucking you. That's the deal, that's the fuckin' deal!"

On TV, again the face of Cate Burns.

60

A man's bare back is on camera. He's arguing with a small crowd of media that seem to have flocked from nowhere. Senator G.B. has been cornered by *City Flash*, again, as he's about to have his swim at an exclusive sports club. He's screaming, "Are you stalking me? Yes, you've been stalking me, I recognize you, boy. What's with you? What do you have against me? I'm a good Christian, I feel for Germinio's widow, I have no quarrel with his family even if they shot my reputation to pieces, I *am* a good Christian!"

The good Christian looks like he is about to have a heart attack.

The stalker is relentless. "Senator, what about the fact that the deceased exposed your alleged involvement with illegal gambling, that you're possibly one of its big bosses, and that someone, in fact, overheard you threaten to 'mow down any two-bit journalist' who messes with your so-called 'operations'—what do you say to that, Senator?"

The bodyguards come between their boss and the reporter, pushing him back as the senator spits out his rage.

"And Senator, do you think there's any connection between Germinio de Vera's murder and the kidnapping of Cate Burns?"

"How dare you—are you implying—?"

"And what about the rumor that innocent people are being harassed because of this series of crimes?" Back and back, the reporter is pushed by the bodyguards—he falls into the pool.

On screen Eugene Costa's face bobs in the water, gasping for air.

Lydia de Vera watches this face from her bed. Get out of the water before you drown, she wants to scream. She remembers the earnest face at the wake, the hand quick with the microphone. He asked the senator about the Pizza Hut man, and her husband. Only a boy, a brave fool. Don't drown, please it's not worth it, don't let your loved ones drown.

61

The women are huddled together before a stack of lantern paper. The candle is lit again. Nena can't keep still. Up and down she rubs her legs under the house-dress, then stops at the hem, twisting it. The twisting is echoed in her gut, but she must be calm, so she won't drown. She must talk normally about the boy they're waiting for.

"*Papel de Japon*—red, green." She tries to explain Noland's choice of Japanese paper in Christmas colors. "No pink, no blue, no yellow—red, green, Noland like." She lays a piece of each color on Cate's hands. "Christmas color," she says. "You like?"

Cate touches the other's hand. "I like, yes."

Nena whispers, "Noland like... Noland like you— you like?"

Cate nods her head. "Yes, I like your son, he's a good boy. He'll be okay. He's just late, a bit late." How lame she sounds. How to believe herself, now that she's wondering about the murdered man, how the boys were there with her then, how they saw it too—what if, oh

God! Should she ask Nena about *that time,* and whether—but what if they're in it?

"Yes, Noland *septy-septy....*" Safety-safety wherever he is right now, Nena hopes. She searches the white woman's face. "You sad...like me...no son, no husband...he die?"

Cate is silent. Her own stories jostle each other inside; she's sinking under their weight. If only she hadn't woken up, couldn't remember. She hears the question again: "He die?" The man back home who did not want *it*?

Nena's eyes are fixed on her face, keen for an answer, but Cate is afraid to open her mouth; she can't trust what might come out. Instinctively she passes a hand over her belly, swallows tears. Her wretchedness is an imposition here, but she can't help hearing him now. Their last conversation.

"It's too sudden, Cate, and unfair. I never agreed to it. It will turn our lives upside down. And your future— you've just started your thesis. It's bad timing, especially now that we're fighting this merger with another department. I'm so stressed out, you know, and you too—it will be too much stress for both of us. Think of the poor child, and your health." So she packed for a Christmas holiday, alone with *it*. He wanted a termination.

He die? No, it die.

"He die?" Again Nena asks.

Cate nods. What satisfaction to wish him dead.

Nena nods too. She makes a decision. From underneath the red and green Japanese paper, she retrieves a notebook. She holds it for a bit, still unsure, then hands it to Cate.

The angels hold their breath. You're not supposed to tell, it's a secret.

"No touch, no see...I touch, I see...you, Noland like...you okay touch, you okay see."

Cate stares at the notebook's cover of angels and stars.

"He like star, he like angel...guardian angel...." Nena makes a gesture of gathering the angels around the hut. "Make Noland-Nena *septy-septy*." She opens to the first page. It has a blond angel cut out from an old Christmas card. She half smiles. "Noland say...you angel...."

62

The film has just finished and the viewers are making a move to leave. It was a free movie, a local comedy, but no one laughed. Even the wire-man Mang Pedring is here, shoulder to shoulder with Mang Gusting and the twins, Vic and Vim. Lisa too, crouched close to her one-time flame, who doesn't look at her now, what with his heartbreak over Hong Kong. Manang Betya leans against her, wondering if luck could be turned around this late. She checked a while ago, and yes the bulldozer is still there.

"Seen them lately?"

"Who, Helen?"

"Nena and Noland. I'm terribly worried about them. You think they're away, went home to the province maybe? But where's their province? I never really asked...you know, *City Flash* said it's maybe street kids...." She lets this dangle, waits for the others' responses.

"Oh-oh," Lisa begins, clutching her chest. "Maybe they think street kids live here, just because we're squatters—"

"I'm not," Manang Betya protests. "I have a proper home and work. By the way," she says, taking out the little *jueteng* notebook from her pocket, "I have a tip for all of you—we can change our luck with a winning combination, you know."

"Aw, shuddup!" It's Mang Pedring, knotting and unknotting his hands. Some hours ago, a plainclothes policeman cornered him while he was tinkering with the wires behind the nearby hardware store. "Aha," the man said. "Going for it again?" He hid his pliers quickly but the man said he could report this freeloading on someone else's circuit, and by the by, tell us about your friends over there, pointing to the intersection. He demanded stories, conspiracies that led to the kidnapping of the American. At a loss, the wire-man soon promised the cop he would find out, but please no reports. Now he's watching each of his neighbors, for any possible story, any possible culprit.

He starts with the lantern maker, who still owes him three hundred. "You, Vim, you were there when it happened, and you helped that man who was shot at the wheel. How come you know him?"

Vim is shocked at the accusation. "I did not know him, I saw him shot!"

"And you were the first to report about the American."

"Lay off my brother." Vic turns on the wire-man. "You know he was bashed because he told the police what he saw—he still has the bruises to prove it. Use your eyes and your stupid head."

"Yes, he was trying to help, foolishly I must say," Manang Betya adds.

"And now we're all under suspicion, under threat, with that *putang 'nang*, that son-of-a-whore bulldozer about to mow us all down," Mario whines. "You and your big mouth, Vim, if you hadn't—"

Vic hits him.

The women crouch in the corner, Lisa starts to weep, Mario keeps swearing, *putang ina*, he's lost a tooth, but he doesn't have the will to hit back, not now anyway. He eyes the twins, rubbing his cheek. Maybe they know something.... They all size each other up, wondering what stories they can tell the soldiers so they'll go away and take their bulldozer with them.

Every look resurrects old grudges. I suspect Manang Betya pocketed my winning once. That Lisa hijacked my laundry customer; and she's done it again to that poor Nena. Ah, Mang Gusting has always turned up his nose at me, just because he's got dollars from Hong Kong. Wonder what he knows, wonder what she's really up to, wonder what they're hiding.

The heart of terror is Machiavellian, and in it is the power of story.

Outside there are no firecrackers, no carols, no karaoke, no blaring trumpets. Unusual two days before Christmas, and all the huts are closed. So are the lantern stalls. It's never been this dark.

"Do you think we're people?" The question breaks the terrified spell. It's Lisa, now chewing her nails.

"What do you mean?"

"They don't think we're people," she whispers.

"No, they do ... we're just nothing people, that's all."

Everyone chews on the thought of being nothing. "Shouldn't we start packing?" Vim rises, his voice shaky. "You know ... just in case...."

"Aw, come off it," Manang Betya scolds, then solemnly begins. "I have a solution," and she takes out her bookie's notes. "I prayed for it, divined it, you bet. Quite simple, it's like inverting bad luck. Now, when was the date of the shooting, the 19th, now add that number to Christmas Day, 25, and..." She whispers into each woman's ear what other numbers to rumble, to win over bad luck. Then she waves her notebook in the air, weaving magic with her story of luck. The men are drawn in, wanting to be part of the action, except for the twins who walk out.

"Oh-oh, yes-yes." Lisa is convinced, taking out a twenty from her pocket and handing it over.

But Helen is less gullible. In fact, she's shocked. "*Dios ko*, how could you let murder and kidnapping in on luck? That's inviting the devil!"

"No, we're scaring the devil away, we're letting the angels rescue us—don't forget we're adding the date of Christmas, 25, so there!"

"No, Manang Betya, these days, real luck is if you find that Cate, then you get the reward."

"Yes, yes, that reward." The others nod, suddenly dreamy.

"Heaps and heaps, I'm sure," Lisa figures.

"And in dollars," Manang Betya chimes in, pressing her luck for more bets. "I tell you, we just need to rumble the numbers for one good luck and we break this dry spell," and she waves her notebook again, amen, amen.

"But street kids, imagine that—no, it's not possible." Helen is about to say more, but shuts her mouth. There was a stranger, a boy wandering around here, he kicked the dog, he went into there one time—she looks out to Nena's hut. It's still shut, still looking empty.

63

Across the tracks the women look at the notebook open on the floor. On its last page, away from all the drawings, is a tabloid clipping from six years ago. It's a photo of a young Nena with four-year-old Noland. Both are looking straight at the camera, the mother with apprehension, the boy curiously.

WIDOW OF SHOT FARMER CRIES FOR JUSTICE

The caption stares Cate in the face.

"My son . . . he see bang-bang. . . ."

WIDOW OF SHOT FARMER. . . .

It steals her breath.

"He see fall, Cate . . . he see father . . . fall. . . ."

In the dark, the secret grows. It finds each corner, invades even her mouth. Cate wants to say sorry forever. She wants to weep with this woman for a long, long time.

"Please-please, Cate Burns, no-go, no-go, no police, no uniforms. . . ."

The angels hear a soft crying.

DECEMBER 23

64

The tracks are deserted, the huts closed. At the intersection, a taxi deposits a boy clutching two bags. He's wearing a new shirt and his first pair of long pants. He seems disoriented. It's dark but on the horizon the sky glows from the city lights. Framed by this glow, the small figure in the middle of the tracks looks eerie. The silent row of huts and the stretch of steel seem to converge toward him, in him. All of this still life.

There's a drummer boy in one bag, food in the other. There's a hundred-dollar bill in one pocket folded neatly over a photo torn from a newspaper, and two five-hundred-pesos in the other.

All dark, the huts look strangely alike. Which is the hut of angels?

He walks a few more paces. He smells of fresh hotel soap and some sweet lotion. His skin is soft from it. He stares at his feet. New shoes too. Black leather. Christmas has come early for him.

He keeps staring at his feet. They made marks on the man's chest when he asked him to stand there for a long time. Stand still. Don't cover yourself, don't be shy. He felt dizzy with the blinking lights. The man took many pictures. He offered many gifts. He spoke all the time in an unfamiliar tongue. His voice was gentle. His hands too when he showed him how to stand, sit, lie down, or look, and when he washed him. He took more pictures in the bath.

The boy shuffles on. Each step is an effort, as if it were his first.

What will his mother say?

His feet feel strange in the shoes.

Will she like him this way?

His pants are too long, he steps on them.

Will she ask?

His body feels strange, dizzy, inside out.

Will the angel ask?

She has a real name now; he has her picture.

He reaches the creek, stands before it in his newness, like a cutout from another story. He softly tiptoes toward the hut; it looks like the right one. He sits at the door. He looks up, searching for stars. There are none. He closes his eyes to make them appear.

The comic strip is not only empty. Each box is black.

65

Elvis and Bobby Cool are sitting on a bench overlooking Manila Bay. Above them, a lit flower lantern. Higher up, the morning star. It's 4 a.m. and in every church around the country the pre-dawn mass has begun. Baywalk is nearly empty of holidaymakers. Except for the late-night-to-early-morning lovers and a confused drunk, the strip is peaceful. But not Elvis. He's seething. He's lost his cap; the cockiness is gone. He's all vulnerable rage, his skin burning, his heart cold. "Fuck you, Bobby, you agreed to leave Noland out of this. You weren't to touch him—you promised!"

Bobby is calm, his voice soft and reassuring. "Aw, simmer down. No one touched him. It was only pictures. He's hit the jackpot for so little work. He was paid very well, even got a big tip. He has plenty of money for Christmas, for his sick mother. What are you complaining about?"

Elvis chokes on his words. He swings at the pimp, hitting him right on the mouth.

Bobby is shocked. His lip is cut, there's blood.

"We're finished, Bobby."

It takes a moment for the man to comprehend what's happened. He looks at the blood on his hand and snaps. He hits the boy square on the face. The boy sprawls on the ground howling, hand on an eye that feels dislodged from its socket. The man kicks him. The small body rolls farther away with the impact. He kicks him again, harder. The boy curls up. The man grabs him by the shirt so that it rips at the collar. He pulls him close and spits out his contempt. "Don't forget, I picked you up from the gutter, I clothed you, I fed you—I saved you! And now you hit me, huh? You ungrateful wretch, you little shit, you whore!" He lets go, then starts to walk away. "So we're finished?" he yells. "See what happens, see how hunger suits you—then you'll come crawling back."

Elvis crouches against the sea wall, sobbing, "I'm going to kill you, I'm going to kill you."

Behind him, the sea is calm, the sky just lightening. Even the waves are not yet fully awake. Soon the first metro aide comes sweeping the street. He asks Elvis if he's okay. Elvis screams at him to fuck off.

66

The women speak to Noland, but he seems not to hear them. He is dizzy inside out. He is here and not here. The room is spinning, the star lanterns are dancing, but when he shuts his eyes, he sees only a strip of black boxes, the black bleeding into each other. All starless night, all nothing.

Above him the cherub looks on, still blissful and as helpless as sooty Saint Michael with his raised sword fixed on the wall. Like Saint Raphael, who can only imagine clutching his fish a little tighter, and nothing more. Like the angel at the door, wishing she had kept it tightly closed between the boy and the world. There is nothing anyone can do against being fixed in one place for the rest of one's life. The gods are in heaven, the mortals on earth.

"Ay, my son, my son!" his mother wails, as if he has died. She's clutching him to her breast, can't let go, even as the other woman tries to help him onto the mat. "Hush, hush," she says. "Lay him down, Nena, lay him down."

"What happened to you, who did this? Are you hurt, did they hurt you? Ay, ay, what did they do to you?"

"Nena...please, let's settle him first."

Shock. The boy's in a state of shock, Cate is sure, but she can't quite understand the new clothes and shoes, the sweet scent, the expensive toy, the food. Maybe nothing really happened, nothing bad...and yet there's another voice sneaking into her head. What if? No, don't go there, don't.

Noland keeps his eyes shut. His mother is angry and he can't tell her anything now, never. He knows a story that can never be told. Because it confuses him. Because he's ashamed. Because he's no longer himself. He feels his shoes being slipped off his feet. What if they see the man's chest on his soles? His shirt is unbuttoned, and his pants. No, no, I don't want you to see me. His mother's sobbing hurts his ears.

Nena checks her son's body for marks, frantically turning him this way and that. It's difficult. He's curled up tight on the mat. Only when a blanket covers him does he relax and fall asleep.

"Nena...Nena...let's leave him alone, let him rest...."

"Ay, Cate . . . me no understanding. . . ."

The women speak in whispers as they go through his things. Each item is a clue for the mother, a stab into her breast. She reverts to her own language, still addressing Cate, who hears her tone clearly, her intent.

"This toy, Cate . . . it looks very expensive. . . ."

"Nena, maybe he was with a friend . . . or a relative?" This sounds so lame.

"And his clothes . . . they're new . . . and the shoes. . . ."

"Christmas gifts maybe from—from—"

"What's this?" Nena has found the two five-hundred-peso bills.

"From—from lantern sales maybe?"

"And this?"

It's the hundred-dollar bill this time. They stare at it, search for a reason.

"That Elvis—that devil, that scum." Hasn't she suspected—*Dios ko,* if she goes to the end of this thought, she'll die.

Very soon she finds Cate's photo folded under the bill. Her fears take another route.

67

The angels look more cheerful. They have no choice. The morning begins to stream into the hut. But the women are grim; they have stopped talking, each alone in their thoughts. When Nena discovered Cate's photo, she kept the Amerkana at arm's length. She's the root of all this, she's a bad-luck woman. Soon the police, the uniforms will come, and it will be over like last time. It will end. The poor have wretched endings every day. Why is that?

Nena has become catatonic like her son, her house-dress riding up her hip, revealing a sight that shocks Cate. Below the tattered panties, all the way down the thighs, scars, then the misshapen knees, the crooked calves. She's crouched at her son's feet, her eyes never leaving his face.

Cate shivers in her corner. There's something about those legs, the violent ugliness of—"an accident"? "You must eat. I'll make breakfast. Yes, you watch over him, but you must eat," she blurts out, rising with a sickly feeling in her gut. But there are only the empty packets of Milo and cheese, and very little water left in the pail in the corner. They finished the bread yesterday. She notes the contents of the bag on the floor, but does not dare touch them. Her stomach grumbles. Chocolate bars, cookies and nuts, two apples, an orange juice. Not local brands. Bought at random in a supermarket? No, hotel food, but they'll never know.

"You must eat something, Nena."

Nena doesn't budge.

Cate wants to come close and pull the housedress down, but the mat where she used to lie is strange territory now. A refuge for mother and son, and she is the intruder.

The boy turns and groans. Both women quickly bend

over him, their breaths held. Was that a word? Did he speak?

He raises a hand and Cate instinctively grasps it. Nena tries to push her away, but she hangs on, clutching the cold fingers, blabbering her anguish.

In the dark in his head, Noland hears it. "Noland... Noland... I like your angels... your angels, Noland."

68

By late afternoon, Nena opens the door. Light floods in. The endless night has abruptly turned into day.

"You go."

"But Nena...."

Only a few paces, and freedom. She'll walk away, go to her embassy, have a shower. Oh to feel clean again and have a proper toilet, not the biscuit tin organized by Nena for her sake.

Nena keeps waving Cate away, then suddenly stops, hesitates. She takes one of the five-hundreds from beside the boy and hands it to her. She motions to the open door. "You go."

She'll go to a hotel, maybe fly to an island; there are many beautiful islands here. She'll have her holiday. She'll put this behind her, everything—this never happened. How can she even think like this?

"Go!"

Cate gets on her knees, crouching too. "Thank you, Nena... but maybe first you should—"

The finger that points to the door is imperious, but the rest of her is broken. She looks older in the full light, skeletal. And the boy, how still.

Bad-luck woman, why did you come? Nena stares into the blue eyes welling with tears. Her own fill too; the tug of grief runs between them, and much more. Pasts so estranged and futures that will never touch again. But here, they are irrevocably bound. Perhaps this is something they know but must deny so they can let the other go. It is possible. Behind tears, the other's face blurs. It could be just any face now.

"Maybe you should—"

"Please go."

Cate takes the money, murmuring her thanks, and steps out the door. She looks up and down the strip of slums, all the salvaged refuse of a city raised into homes, into lives leaning against each other, trusting this sheer effort to stand and remain standing.

Two naked little boys gawk at the white giant in a brightly flowered dress that's too small for her. Across the tracks, Helen stares in disbelief. The white woman meets her stare, is about to say something, then returns to the hut. She shuts the door. "Here," she says, returning the money. "I think we should take him to a doctor."

69

Helen takes the two boys by the hand, away from the door. She puts a finger to her lips—don't tell anyone—then sends them home. She looks around. Did anyone see what she saw? My God, it's her neighbors then. Ah, I knew it in my gut—and maybe that strange boy who visits them, and the Pizza Hut man? They're all in it together. Who would ever think? But that Cate—she's sure it's her from the photo—she looks okay, no sign that she's been shot. How very white. Whiter than on TV.

Helen stands in the middle of the tracks, raises both hands to heaven. Thanks be to God, we're saved, we're all safe now. But should she tell her neighbors? She quickly returns to her hut. Her husband Mario is out today. She can't tell him anyway. She shouldn't tell anyone yet—but what if? No, how can she be wrong—the proof was there, staring her in the face a minute ago. No wonder Nena looked terrified whenever the police were mentioned. But wasn't she always fearful, even before?

She remembers how they arrived two years ago with nothing but that boy's cart, a few plastic bags, and that junk of a TV. They parked across from her house, among the garbage, and slept in the cart for the first night. The mother talked all the time, as if she were talking for the boy, who never spoke. Helen couldn't help herself. She went over and chatted. The mother told her their names and a vague story about losing their house. Then she grew as silent as her son. Since then Helen has known nothing more about them. She suspects the poor boy isn't quite right in the head, that's why he can't speak. He stares at her in that strange way, unblinking and serious and sad; it makes her look away.

Who would ever think — but you never know with people these days. Murderers can look like saints. But there's still this war inside her. If she rings the authorities, that would be betrayal. If she doesn't, there's the bulldozer. She sorts the videos on the floor and turns on the TV to drown her doubts and another thought, a little spark of hope that she must extinguish — but how can she think this now?

She looks around the hut with its half a concrete wall. The rest is saved bits and pieces from everywhere, but it has enough room for the video viewers, even a couch. Its bedroom and kitchen are set apart by plastic curtains. And it has a large TV screen and a video — who knows, they might even switch to DVD? Theirs is a hut that's on its way to becoming a proper house if they get lucky — and what if they do get lucky?

70

City Flash has a special news edition. The Christmas crime is now the most celebrated case of the year. The whole country is agog over the bizarre whodunit.

The anchorwoman goes through the twists and turns of

the plot with convincing realism so that most viewers feel this story is now their own, that they could be at risk if they ordered a Pizza Hut delivery, that poor Cate is their very own heroine, and that they must watch out for street kids and keep their car windows shut at those busy intersections, and perhaps it's a good idea to clean up that part of the city—you never know what terrorists it harbors. But some viewers are appalled that the journalist's murder has been sidelined by this fixation on that American and on the specter of terrorism against the U.S. Angry debates have been brewing around the nation, so *City Flash* has gathered a panel "to chat in the spirit of peace and goodwill."

Helen stops sorting videos. She sits on the couch and watches keenly, cell phone in hand. She must get those special numbers to ring. She's sure they'll show them again on the screen.

The panel includes a priest, the president's press secretary, a journalist, a political analyst from the state university, and an American official. So the discussion is fair and square. The studio is crawling with media. The case has alerted the foreign press and has been growing a life of its own in the other side of the globe, where the husband of the lost American has broken down on American TV.

Young Eugene Costa is squeezed between two American journalists.

Father Ruben Santos opens the panel, and rightly so, as he explains. "This isn't just about murder or abduction or terrorism. It's an issue for soul-searching in this season of peace and goodwill. I know the radicals among you will think I sound like I'm giving a sermon, but I'm just presenting the tragic core of this case: the loss of peace. Think of the violence in our streets. Then there's the loss of goodwill. There's so much bickering among us Filipinos when we should be asking, why are our children involved."

"With all due respect, Father, while I agree with you, isn't it better for us to look at the root of the loss of peace and goodwill, and the terrible plight of our children?" Mary Ann Fuentebella, a writer for one of the major dailies, wrings her hands before the audience. "The reality is that no one's safe in this country, not our children, not our journalists, or our tourists, because of the political machinations of a rotten system. Why do you think Germinio de Vera was shot? Why do you think we have street children? Why are we murdered if we expose the stink of the system—tell me if this is not terrorism. Filipinos know terror in their own homes, in their own streets."

Father Santos clears his throat for a riposte, but the only foreigner in the panel gets in first. Colonel David Lane is the reluctant American official. He never wanted to come, but he's the public face of this American case, so he might as well make an effort. "Miss Fuentebella, I totally agree with your point about home-based terrorism and of course the United States sympathizes with you on this—has worked in fact with your government in the *Balikatan* program. We're on the same side, more so now that terrorism is a global issue that we should—"

"Colonel, why don't you review your history?" she

cuts in. "Listen to this. The Philippines: nearly four hundred years under Spain, forty years under *your* America, three years under Japan—passed from hand to hand like chattel! And of course, forever under governments run by Filipinos who have terrorized their own people. Please, Colonel, don't dare lecture us on terrorism."

"I'm sorry, Miss Fuentebella, but the United States is not lecturing you on terrorism. As you may appreciate, politically motivated violence has new dimensions, so the contemporary use of the word 'terrorism' is entirely different from the old definition—"

She's even more incensed. "So who defines it now? You think you have a patent on the word?"

"Please hear me out, okay? If there are terrorist speculations about the abduction and possible shooting of an American national, it's because of the previous American hostage crises in Mindanao—I'm sure you're aware of *that* history. It's because we've suffered from 9/11 and have grown acutely sensitive to any untoward actions against our citizens."

The woman swings toward him, her body making its own argument. "9/11 is tragic—any senseless death is tragic. But do you ever reflect on both sides of the equation? The problem with America is that it always paints itself as victim if not liberator or peace broker—never as an aggressor!"

Quickly the president's press secretary makes peace. "Colonel Lane, we feel for that great tragedy of your people." Venancio Reyes outdoes the American's apologetic tone. "I truly understand the unfortunate repercussions of 9/11, as evidenced by your government's response to this current case, and of course the earlier American hostage crises in Mindanao are crucial to this current case. Let me assure you that the president herself has promised full support for Cate Burns. These are stressful times and, under stress, of course we act accordingly."

"Like our government giving priority to a lost American—more than its own citizens? Like taking a combat helicopter on a city tour? Like threatening the most helpless with demolition? Now, think about that, Colonel. We're ready to erase the lives of our own people, for your sake!" Miss Fuentebella flings her bitterness at the crowd, her face contorting with the effort. "But what's new? All these years we've always kissed the ass of the imperialist."

Everyone is silenced. The university professor decides against speaking. He's bitterly disappointed. He came here with high hopes. No grandstanding, please. Don't sabotage our chance to talk about this intelligently, to gain some political clout for the deceased.

The silence is only a beat. Soon the press are shooting questions and hardly anyone can be heard in the din. Eugene finds himself being quizzed by the American journalists.

"Who's that?"

"The lady has balls!"

On her couch, Helen feels totally excluded. She can barely understand the discussion. The panel is in English.

71

The women stare at the American hundred-dollar bill and Cate's photo. Does the boy's condition have something to do with her? And what did *they* do to him? *They* or *he*? The Pizza Hut man. And the gifts are a bribe for — the women make sure the door is firmly shut. Nena refuses to take the boy to a doctor. Cate cringes at the blame in her eyes.

There's a knock. The women look at each other anxiously.

"They've come," Nena whispers, crawling back to her son, but she's stopped midway by the voice outside.

"You okay, Noland?"

Elvis!

"So it's that devil after all, I'll make him pay for this." Nena lets him in, quickly grabbing his feet, tripping him. On the floor, she hits him, waves the money at him. "What's this? You know about this, don't you? What have you done to my son? What happened to my son?"

"No, Nena, let the boy go, let him tell us." Cate tries to intervene. She notes the swollen eye and the ripped collar, the grimy shirt, the bruised knees.

"I'm sorry, Noland, I'm sorry, he didn't hurt you, did he, tell me he didn't, Noland, tell me." He wants to get to the mat but Nena pins him down, pummelling him with her fists.

"You're going to tell me what happened to my son, you're going to pay for this, you scum."

"It wasn't me, Aling Nena, it wasn't me."

Unable to understand the exchange, Cate tries to get Nena off the boy. "What's he saying? Let him tell us, leave him alone. He's hurt, can't you see? What happened? Please tell us. Was it—was it because of the shooting?"

"I hit him, Noland," Elvis calls out to his friend, who is just waking up. "I hit him right-smack on the face, I hit him for you—but he didn't hurt you, did he? Bobby said he wasn't meant to. It's true, isn't it—isn't it?"

Nena's fury fills the hut. She wails curses, she damns him to hell.

Outside the train passes. They barely hear each other.

The knowledge rips the mother apart. She drives him out of the hut, screaming, "You little whore, you little whore!"

On the mat the boy wants to tell them it's not him, not his friend, but he can't tell, ever. He closes his eyes again. *I know a story you don't know.*

72

I'm like everyone. I'm turning with a thousand lights. I'm just another light. If only he could believe it.

Elvis is in the sky. The Ferris wheel studded with rainbow lights turns and turns. It blurs all the riders beyond recognition. It's only a lightstreaky wheel to those below, perhaps a whirling pattern of shining stones to the stars above. It's competition, a brighter constellation.

Elvis kept walking when he left the hut, roaming list-lessly, retracing the route he and Noland took when they sneaked away. He ended up at Star City. He smirked at the guard, who didn't recognize him, though he stared at his black eye, even asked if he's okay. He played the games. He did the roller coaster, then the bumper cars. He bought himself a new cap and a toy re-volver; he stole a pocket knife. He fancied himself armed to the teeth. I am deadly.

He is above the city now. No one can hurt him up here. He wishes he could believe this. But there's this pain ex-panding in his chest, as if it's about to explode. Of course it's where Bobby kicked him. Up here, he can't see the hotel where he took them. He can't see the intersection. They don't exist. Down there are just lights. He can't see the pimp who's now in a bar convincing another drunk that he saves children from the gutter. He can't see that in many homes the television flashes the great news of the season. A concerned Filipino has reported a sighting of the lost American. Cate Burns has been found.

73

The intersection is crawling with uniforms. Two bull-dozers, a crane, armored cars, and an ambulance are on stand-by, and the sirens are wailing. The Huey hovers above, an angel sending the air into a terrified spin.

"We're back at the scene of the crime." Eugene tries to talk over the drone vibrating even his teeth. He's whipped about, his microphone nearly slipping from his hands. "Cate Burns is being held in one of these huts. Cate Burns is about to be rescued. The Philippine National Police, along with the military and some U.S. officials, are working together tirelessly in this dramatic culmination of a story that has filled the last few days."

The city is glued to the screen. This is the most exciting reality TV, and at Christmas too. The mystery is about to be solved. The story will have a true Christmas ending. Salvation.

There's a shot of the blinking stars, the slums, the residents trying to run to or from their homes but cordoned off by the authorities, then the frenzied media and the growing curious mob that is almost impossible to contain. Eugene rushes closer to where the Special Action Force spills from a van, in dark camouflage and helmets and masks, assault rifles at the ready. He's pushed back, he keeps reporting. "We understand that late this afternoon, a call was made to the police about a sighting of the missing American. And the initial speculation is right. Street children were involved in her disappearance. But right now, what we're seeing is the biggest breakthrough in this Christmas crime."

Lydia de Vera is watching her screen, feeling sick. The rescue of the American is the biggest breakthrough? How can you say that?

Assault rifles slip from hut to hut. A gloved hand

draws a circle in the air, then a thumbs-up sign, a nod from a dark mask, all precise speeches in eerie silence.

Around their home theater, Senator G.B. and his family pin their hopes on this breakthrough. Street kids. He'll be exonerated.

The faces of Mikmik and her gang flash past, their terror leaping out of the screen.

The American embassy officials are still at work, glued to this event, which they were alerted to early tonight.

The lantern twins are crouched at their door, hands on their heads before an armed officer, and the camera moves on, over an array of lives, of histories reduced to frame after frame.

The Philippine president and her press secretary are also watching with great relief, as is the whole nation.

Finally *the* hut. The door is kicked, the assault rifles barge in, then the screams.

On the other side of the globe, Americans are also fixed before their screens, captured by this spinning web. Now they'll know the story. They're about to meet Cate Burns and her abductors, maybe even the Pizza Hut terrorist man. No one blinks. This is *their* story now. In no time the screen is filled by a startled-looking white woman being strapped to a stretcher. She's struggling? She's screaming at her rescuers? "Listen to me, this is a mistake, I said listen to me!" She's spirited off screen, then another screaming woman is bodily lifted by one of the uniforms. Behind her is a boy looking dazed, holding onto his *Tagaligtas,* his armed "Savior."

Is that the street kid? Where's the Pizza Hut terrorist man?

The woman is lifted away from the boy. She's kicking, sobbing, pleading for the boy.

Ah, the mother. The mother and her son.

The public search their screens for that ferocious monster lurking inside, waiting until it's dragged out of the hut. Nothing.

Is that all?

74

The angels have been orphaned, just like that, their purpose lost. There's no one to guard now. Saint Michael will never use his sword, even if he once vanquished the revolt of angels in heaven. Saint Raphael will be perpetually pinned onto the wall, as is his healing fish. He's the patron of the young, but not today. The cherub, the winged child, won't guarantee safety. He's meant to live in the safest place in heaven, so he will never fly from the roof. And the angel guarding the door will let in the next troop of uniforms.

"My God, Chief, just look at this!" one of the forensics team whispers, hesitating at the door of the hut that isn't quite empty. Roberto Espinosa enters before the others, all gaping. A reverent quietude washes over them, as if they've walked into a cathedral. The flickering heart of the tree makes the stars and angels tremble among the shadows of the men.

"It could be . . . that the boy's mad."

The remark breaks the spell and the men get to work, discovering key items that will later fuel various media spins, depending on who's writing for whom. They find Cate's bloodstained clothes. Then the money and Cate's photo from the paper. Then Noland's notebook, which is scanned with care. They see angels and stars, the endless comic strips flowing into each other. They find the tabloid clipping about the death of a farmer six years ago. He killed his landlord, hacked him to death, before he was shot while escaping.

With each page that's turned, the angels want to look away. Each of the boy's secrets is out now, each desecrated by the hands of strangers.

There is one peculiar drawing of a star. It fills the page and is framed by a circle. Each of the star's five points is also encircled. In each circle is a pasted picture: the boy they arrested, his mother, a man (is he the Pizza Hut man?), then another boy (the report said there were two of them), and the last circled point is still empty—but of course there's the picture of the American freshly torn from a newspaper to the same size as the other photos. She is the fifth point.

A star has five lights. Noland thinks it so it must be true. Angels live in stars, with fire in their chests. So when they breathe, the sky twinkles.

If only the angels can tell the stories that Noland tells himself.

In the way the star is drawn and decked, it looks like a—what do you call it, a mandala? Is this evidence of a cult? Was the American abducted by a cult? And the journalist shot by their hitman? Are the boys working for a terrorist cult?

They bag all the evidence. They must find that other boy.

75

The chief examines the pasted angels, holding his lighter close to their faces when he can. The full spectrum intrigues him: from smiling innocence to bliss to vengeful conviction. He waits until everyone else has left, and turns his attention to the tree. He's fascinated. What a clever light contraption.

The candle inside the milk can splutters and he reaches in, trying to rekindle it with his lighter. This is how David Lane finds him, like a child secretly fixing up his tree. He withdraws his hand, embarrassed, and angry that he is. The candle dies. The two men face each other in the dark. Then the American moves forward to restore the light himself and extends his hand. "I'm David, David Lane."

"I know, Colonel," the chief says, carefully enunciating

the last word and ignoring the offered hand. "And I'm Roberto Espinosa of Special Projects. We're in charge of the case."

"Of course," David is quick to confirm.

The two men stare at the candle trying to keep its light, the brave wick not quite succeeding, then David breaks the silence. "Smoke?" He offers the man his pack while lighting up.

"Don't burn the evidence to the ground, Colonel," he says, blowing out the candle completely. "Let's go outside."

David feels chastised. He bites back a cutting riposte. He can understand the other man's belligerence. He'd hate anybody on his own turf too. He puts out his light, saying, "Whatever you say," and follows the older man, who retorts, "That's right, whatever I say."

Outside his phone rings. The Filipino officer takes the call and the American waits, keeping his distance, trying not to cover his nose against the smell of human excrement rising from the creek. The flashing lights from a police car help him to make out the other: gray hair, slight build, barely reaching his shoulders. He catches an expletive and the word "senator," and sees the man looking at him with even more contempt.

When the call ends he says, "I'm ordered to accommodate your needs, Colonel, because we must stand shoulder to shoulder." He walks off briskly, without even looking at the American, through the babble of relief traveling the tracks. Ay, thank God, it's over, the culprits have been arrested and we're saved, we're safe again. After the phone call, for Roberto, "safe" will always be a pretend word.

76

"Of course I was shocked. They're my neighbors, you see. They seemed to be good people. They came here two years ago. Nena can't walk, and her son Noland is mute. She used to wash clothes for Mrs. Sy across the highway and he makes those little paper lanterns, sells them at the intersection—but the other boy, I don't know about him, though I saw a strange boy going in there. He had an argument with my husband a few days ago, I remember now. Plenty of attitude, that boy."

Eugene is interviewing Helen, who has much to say. Her heart is pounding. She can't believe she's on *City Flash*. She must ask if they'll replay this, so she can watch. Imagine if her neighbors were watching now.

Her neighbors *are* watching, live. They've flocked around, wanting to get on TV too. The crew fans the excitement, the camera lights ease the darkness within. Mikmik and her gang make faces behind Helen, trying to catch the camera's eye.

"You live just across from their hut," Eugene says. "So how well do you know them?"

Helen hesitates, then, "Tell me, did they hurt Cate? I mean, I still can't believe they'd hurt her. They're actually very peaceful folks, though you never know these days...." Her voice trails off; she stares at her feet. "No, I don't really know them, they're just neighbors."

"You said they've lived here for two years. Did you notice anything strange about them, or any strange happenings around here?"

"Well... that Noland, he stares in that strange way, if you know what I mean." She makes a gesture to indicate that he's not right in the head. She thinks of Nena's ugly legs. "It's sad, you know."

"Tell us again how you saw Cate Burns for the first time."

"Well, she was just standing there, this afternoon." She points to the hut crawling with police. "I couldn't believe my eyes, you see—then she went back into the hut and shut the door. Very strange."

"And you rang the police. There is the reward, as you're aware."

"Of course, it's not about the reward," she protests. Should she tell him about the bulldozer? Doesn't he know? Then she finds the best answer. "Young man, it's really about being a good Christian this Christmas. Christ saved us, right? So I save the American. It's what any good Christian will do."

"Thank you for talking to us here on *City Flash*."

Then he turns back to the camera to proceed with his report.

"Do you think they'll be all right . . . I mean Nena and Noland?" Helen whispers from behind, but the reporter is already walking away with his crew.

77

He hurts more now that he's back on solid ground, in the park of the fountain and giant lanterns. Earlier he checked his bruises in the toilets at Star City. The one on his chest isn't the shape of a shoe and the pain is deeper and rising, pushing at his ribs. If there were a fairy tale about the ribcage, perhaps he would understand.

Once upon a time in a land far away, there was a ball in a box with slats to peek through. It saw that the world was not good. The seeing hurt it more than the being out there, because it could not do anything. In the box the ball bounced and raged, but still it could not do anything about the world. The bouncing bruised the ball, strained the box to its seams, hurting it too.

The rage kicks in again, making it hard to breathe. Elvis paces. He tries to lose himself in the season's revelry, but he can't, not on solid ground. He sees the sisters who commandeered their cart last night, fast asleep on the mat behind the cars. Around them bliss abounds. He whips out the toy revolver tucked at his waist and aims at the girls—bang-bang! No one bats an eyelash. Happiness is such a deadening thing.

Across the road the church is empty. He plays hide-and-seek with the guards as he slips in. He stops by the sign about not leaving one's things unattended. He shoots it too. He walks to the altar, gun at the ready. He finds the nativity. He comes close, surveys the Holy Family: Mary and Joseph staring at their child, their child staring at him. He aims. The stare does not waver. Still solemn, still knowing. He lowers the gun to his side. His eyes smart, his chest gives.

78

Nena is squatting in a corner, glued to the wall. She is holding her son like a baby. His head is buried on his mother's breast, his body curled. Her head is burrowed between her knees, her legs drawn in to shield him. In the dim light they look like one body, not human, just limbs bound together.

A corridor away a young man crazed by speed is screaming about monsters. The drunks, streetwalkers, and petty criminals arrested for the night scream over his screaming, "Shut up, shut up!" and ask the guard to take this crazy out of here. They get all sorts in this season. But the most precious find is in tight security. Not in a cell but a waiting room without windows. The door is double-locked, an armed guard posted outside. The guard's ears feel the assault even this far away. Why doesn't someone gag that mouth?

Nena thinks of pigs being butchered in the big house, long ago on the farm. They could hear them a long way away. The pain in her legs makes her feel faint. She hushes it, hushes her son, who's beginning to whimper. She whispers his name over and over like a nursery rhyme, and she's returned to his baptism in the village. Her husband insists that he, not his wife, must hold his son in the ritual of naming. He cradles the bawling baby, the weight of a name. *Noland.*

The machinery is rolling. The police are on the case, the military are on the case, and so are the American embassy and the presidential palace. There's no sleep, no relief for the phone lines. In the police compound the notebook has passed between tables and hands, as have the theories and conjectures.

The compound is patrolled by armed men. The blue blinds are drawn. There are armored cars and more armed men outside the gate. Traffic is blocked. The media keep vigil on the other side, some meters from the blocked area. It's not yet midnight.

"What do you think is happening in there?" a journalist asks Eugene Costa. It's the American who stood beside him during the panel. "They can't hold a ten-year-old like that."

"He's with his mother and I was told they're with someone from the DSW," Eugene explains.

"What's that?"

"The Department of Social Welfare—to make sure they're okay."

"And you believe that?"

Eugene can't answer. The American stops asking. There's something companionable about doubt. Strangers feel like old buddies.

"Makes you tired...and angry," Eugene mutters under his breath.

"I know."

The two men sit on the pavement.

The American is first to speak again. "I've followed this case since it broke out. It's incredible, mad. I don't think I can believe anything now."

"I know." Eugene wants to talk about a detail, but it's not news to be reported: the boy looking like he just woke up among the masks and assault rifles. He's holding onto the hand of one of the soldiers. When his mother is taken away screaming, he just keeps holding on.

79

The senator is on the phone. He's growing impatient with this long overseas call. Occasionally he nibbles some low-fat chips. His beer is no longer cold. "Yes, yes, this is a heart-to-heart—senator to senator, okay? I don't want complications and you don't want complications.

This is a local matter, but I'm sure your ambassador will understand—very wise to get her out on the next plane. Great relief for the Burns family, I'm sure—and we're just as relieved that her uncle's on the ball over there. By the way, this Colonel David guy, you think he's okay?"

He listens to the winding tale in the other end, making impatient faces. "I know, I know, but it will still help if you ring your ambassador—yes, as we speak, I'm watching the latest."

The update on the arrest is on the screen that fills a whole wall. His eyes don't leave it. Could it be that the terrorist group Abu Sayyaf has spread its claws beyond the south? Is this "terrorist cult" at the intersection an Abu Sayyaf cell? There's fear of a rescue attack from the terrorist cult. Fuck! Whose spin is that? His *own* journalists must stay on the case.

"How can I forget? Of course, I'll take care of it, amigo."

The den is like an intimate cinema with its home theater, a sprawling bar, and a bed.

"Yes, it's been difficult, the damned media—thanks for your concern."

The beer has gone flat. Senator G.B. throws up his hand in the air, exasperated. "Listen, my reliable sources here tell me it's a cult killing—no, no, not terrorism—that's another media hype. It's safe, yes, your interests are safe here. They're not in Mindanao, remember."

He listens for a moment, then, "Quid pro quo. If you help me, I'll help you—the last thing we want is to complicate the case when we're finally seeing some light." He chuckles at something said in the other line. He lounges on the bed, a squat man who swears by the gym. He strokes his pecs, as if they were a precious pet. "I know, we live in very interesting times—as you do there in America—though we're more interesting here. You'd believe anything here."

G.B. has been making calls since the arrest and even before it. He has friends and those who aren't friends are afraid of him. He knows the perfect pressure points. He frets that he must stay home tomorrow to monitor them. He will miss the gym. Already he feels the protest in his limbs.

"You see, I'm innocent, I'm exonerated, thank God. After all the grief the media have given me—but you'll make that phone call, of course. I'm sure your ambassador will welcome sound advice."

He's comforted by the other's assurance. He changes channel. He has seen enough, talked enough. He's dying for another beer, a very cold beer.

"Yes, I'm fine—and your mining deal, of course. I'll make sure it *is* fine. My Christmas gift . . . of course, I'm a friend." Then suddenly his impatience dissipates. "What—which Celestia? You mean the drug multinational Celestia?" He listens intently.

"A sure bet? When did you know?" His face lights up. "Fantastic! Well, thanks for the tip, amigo. Yes, of course, anytime—and a very merry Christmas to you too."

Suddenly the senator feels his day lifting, his limbs

easing. Ah, some things are better than the gym. He chooses the coldest beer in the fridge, guzzles it. He'll make another phone call, this time to his broker. Two thousand Celestia shares, yes! The beer fizzes in his throat, the figures rise in his head. In this part of the city, there's no need to rumble them for luck.

80

A star is hung at a window too soon. It's not yet whole. The star maker, whose face she can't see, polishes each shell and raises it to her for approval. She inspects it. It's so shiny, like a mirror, she can see herself on it. The shell is glued to the star then they start all over again. Polish, inspect, attach, until the star is finished. Now it lights up, flashing each facet like a giant gem. The star maker is gone. It's just her and the star making prisms. Each facet bears her face. Each has a story of her face.

There's Cate at the airport, staring at a star that blinks like an alarm. Cate awed by the flashing stars at an intersection. Cate on a bed of bloodstained stars. Cate among stars infused with light. Cate inside a star.

The star maker is peeking at her. It's the boy. He breaks into the star to reach for her, but his hand comes out empty and all the little shells are undone. He starts all over again. Cate starts all over again. He polishes each shell, raises it to her for approval and glues it back on. But when they do the next shell, the first comes off. They can't finish the job.

It is a restless dream. Cate begs the boy to please stop, but no sound comes from her mouth.

81

It's only the star at the hospital window. Her half-closed eyes make out the small lantern. She's still groggy from the drug used to settle her. There are murmurs she can't quite make out.

"She wasn't shot, she must have fallen. There's mild concussion, nothing too serious—and she miscarried. There are signs of PTSD, of course. Yes, post-traumatic stress disorder. I suggest we keep this short."

Three figures lean toward her, all soft voiced.

"Welcome back, Cate...I'm Dr. Hill. You have visitors."

"Hello, Cate. We're from the embassy. I'm Bettina and this is David. We're here to make you as comfortable and safe as possible. The ambassador sends her best. She'll do everything she can to help."

All efficient kindness coming to focus: the *mestizo* doctor and two Americans, the consul and the colonel, who have dropped the formalities.

"The hospital is only a few minutes' walk from the embassy, so everything is fine." The consul pats her hand. "If there's anything you need, we're close by. Your backpack's in the closet, all your papers are safe, and we got you some fresh clothes—they're in there too. It's very comfortable here, like a home really." The consul makes a sweeping gesture around the luxurious suite. "I'll leave you with friends now. Someone will stay at the other side, in your private lounge, for as long as you're here—if you need anything. We know you've been through so much. I'm very sorry."

A tear slides down Cate's cheek. The consul grasps her hand. "Oh my dear, it's okay now. You're safe."

Cate notices another man by the window, looking out. He is Filipino, much older, in fact gray, and grim. His shirt reflects the colors of the star above him.

"They're not safe. . . ." she whispers.

"Yes, Cate—did you want something?"

"Nena and Noland, where are they?"

"My dear, everything has been taken care of—"

"Are they okay?" She clutches the arm of the consul, who gently disengages herself.

"We'll be in touch. We'll take care of everything."

As the consul leaves, Cate notes the two Americans in the adjoining lounge. There's another one in the lobby and one parked in the street. This is a private hospital, respected and very discreet.

"Please—we'll keep this short?" the doctor murmurs, checking his watch: an hour before midnight. He shuts the door quietly.

The man at the window pulls up a chair and sits,

facing her this time. He nods at her but doesn't say anything. It's David Lane who proceeds with the necessary business. He can't stop it now, since he was pushed into this bizarre case. His superiors think he's the man for the job. Youthful and unthreatening, a convincing public face. The people's colonel, no less.

"So Cate, you're doing a Ph.D. at Cornell. Literature? I was never any good at it. You like it there? Oh yes, we're practically neighbors by the way. I'm from Ithaca." His smile is disarming.

Who is this man—and that other one?

The American smiles amiably. "Winter can be miserable, I know. Nothing like a break from the cold. So you came for a holiday, landed on the nineteenth—how was the flight?"

"What do you want?"

"I want to help, if you allow me."

"And you are—I didn't catch your name—"

"David—David Lane—from the embassy."

"And who's he?" She points to the man at the window.

"A friend, Roberto Espinosa. Our friend."

The friend nods, forces a smile.

"From the embassy too?"

"He wants to help too. We all want to help."

"You mean, you want to interrogate me." She shuts her eyes, then after a while, "Okay, I'm Cate Burns. I'm here as a tourist. I wasn't shot. I saw *him* shot. I wasn't abducted. I was rescued. That boy and his mother saved my life. If you want to help me, you should—"

"It's just a chat, Cate. Of course, we want to help you."

She opens her eyes again, reaches out to the tall American so neat in his white shirt and crew cut, perfect against the antiseptic walls. "If you want to help, then please tell me where they are. Are they safe?"

The Filipino is all ears. Under the star his sobriety is lit, made colorful.

"That boy's sick, something terrible happened to that boy." She attempts to raise herself from the bed. "He needs help, please."

David grasps the outstretched hand. "Why—what happened, Cate?"

"I—I don't know, you have to find out, you have to help."

"Is he hurt?" David asks. "Did someone hurt him?"

"I think—"

"You think—"

She flops back on the bed, exhausted. In her head Noland is staring from the mat, no longer solemn but with a dark look, full of foreboding, eyes afraid, unrecognizing, as if they've never met before.

"I think...I don't know." She closes her eyes, cups her hands to her ears. Nena's screaming again before those masked men but the boy's silence is louder. It hurts, it hurts her ears.

"Cate, it's okay, it's okay...you're doing fine, Cate, doing fine. Now please tell us about the shooting. This Pizza Hut delivery man or boy—did he shoot at you?"

"No. I already said that."

"Are you sure?"

Cate doesn't answer. She runs through the scene in her head, the sound of shots and she turns around and the man is slumped on the wheel and the motorcycle's coming at her, then she's in the cart and hurting—was she shot at? She can't breathe.

David smiles kindly, murmuring, "No pressure, take your time."

What did his superiors say before he left Iraq? The young colonel was a model soldier, decorated for bravery in Afghanistan, just like his grandfather in the Second World War, though the old man didn't crack up. Fallujah was a shock, but Lane's made some significant contribution, and we must take care of our own. Besides he's damned good with other negotiations, he's psych ops material. He may not be one for the rough and tumble of the field, but he can extricate the truth nicely. Send him for some R and R in the tropics. He'll be okay there for a while.

"Forget the shooter. Where was this boy who saved you, Cate, while all this was happening?"

"He was—with another boy."

The man at the window leans forward. There were two boys, yes.

The colonel nods, then says gently, "And what were these boys doing?"

"They were—they had this cart—"

"A cart—what kind of cart?"

"No, no, they're not what you think—they helped me. They took me to the hut in that cart, they risked their lives, they saved me—" Her voice rises.

"It's okay, Cate, it's okay, I understand."

She grabs his hand. "You must understand, please you must!" She keeps seeing how they held mother and son away from each other, and the rifles pointed at the boy, and his face, his face—her voice keeps rising. "They took care of me, his mother took care of me, I was sick, and I couldn't remember—"

"You're okay, Cate, you're doing fine—what couldn't you remember?"

The door opens; it's the doctor. "I'm sorry, you should go."

David nods at the other man, who stands up reluctantly, still silent. "Take care, Cate. We'll chat again tomorrow. By the way, you should call home—"

"There's no one home."

"I still think you should call your husband."

She's crying now. "They're innocent, it's all a mistake, please help them—they saved my life, I'm telling you, they need help." She's almost screaming. "I just know something bad happened—they need help, they'll get hurt, they're hurt and I—I—" She's completely undone.

The doctor opens the door for the men.

She calls out to them. "Please find out where they are, if they're safe. Please, please ask for me."

82

"Mr. American, please ask for me." In Fallujah, a woman grabbed his hand and wouldn't let go. His men cocked their rifles, ready to frisk her in case this was a terrorist ploy, but she was undaunted. "Ah-med, Ahmed," she kept chanting the name, broken up by her weeping, begging him to ask about her son who'd been arrested for insurgency. Something about her compelled him to listen, to stay a minute too long. Maybe it was her hand around his, that grip of mothers. Then all went wrong. A shot was fired but it was one of his men who fell. A sniper from one of the houses. The next time they were back in the area, she was no longer there, her house was no longer there. But what made the news were the wounded American soldier and the colonel's error of judgment that endangered the lives of his men.

That mother screaming for her son. That hut at the intersection. They too will be lost, but how many will ask about their story?

Please ask for me. David sits in his car outside the hospital, his hands immobile on the wheel. He wonders if he did a survey around the world, how many he would find unable to do their own asking about a missing son. How easy for one query to bear the weight of a life, of many lives—the one asked about, the one asking, the one asked to ask who finds himself unwittingly owning the question, owning the lost one. He hears Cate again, her query. Such desperation to know, as if the boy were her own. He inquired about where they were keeping the boy and his mother, but Roberto Espinosa answered with undisguised contempt. "Of course, you had to do all the talking, Colonel. Shoulder to shoulder? What a joke. The case is not about your American compatriot, it's about my country."

After David left Cate's room, he felt again as if someone had knocked him about. He remembers how he rang his wife all the way from Fallujah, because he could no longer find that mother's house. She had stopped talking to him because of Iraq but for the first time, she took the call. "Come home," she said. "Just come home."

He did, because they sent him home, and there she did not know what to do with him. They did not know what to do with each other. Since then she has acted as if she has been grievously wronged, endlessly complaining that when he's home, he's raring to leave. That he broods. That he drags a shadow around. That he has lost all desire.

David slumps onto the wheel. It receives his wretchedness, like another face that's perpetually hard, undaunted by journeys. *Come home.* Ah, all these wives and mothers waiting, beckoning, as if we've just gone to the corner store on an errand and can easily slip back into their arms, a boy again, enfolded.

83

He was coming home after an interview on a corruption case. The police told her he was eating a pork bun. They found the peelings in the car.

Lydia de Vera turns off the television. It is midnight. There's nothing much to know that she doesn't already know by heart, and she can't bear hearing about the mother and child in custody. All that show of force in case the terrorist cult attempts a rescue—it makes her sick. Her husband would have been there, barging into that police compound, pushing and pushing until he found out the truth. He would have been murdered all over again.

Foolish men. Not for a moment do they think of their wives who will be widows or their mothers who will be childless, but about country and integrity, the bigger picture. Always the home is too small. The heroic resides somewhere else. If not the streets, the halls of government, or a war.

Would they have loved them less if they were not heroes? No. They would have loved them longer.

They had the funeral today, barely a flash in the news. Now she must fold her husband's clothes to give away. At least there's something to do.

DECEMBER 24

84

The morning star is brighter, perhaps because it's Christmas Eve. Though it's only the early hours, pilgrims must be guided to the stable where it all began. But this *first story* is too familiar and the star has long been unmasked as a planet. Pilgrimages no longer end with epiphanies. We know too much now.

One can know too much at twelve years old. Elvis sits on his favorite bench along Manila Bay, opening and closing the stolen pocket knife. He can peer a little now from his left eye. He runs a finger over it to check if the swelling has subsided. The gesture is as slow as his thoughts. He goes through each event since he sneaked away with his friend to Star City. He hasn't slept since then. Each little moment adds up to a lifetime in his head.

He wonders how long Noland was in that hotel room. He comes here for the sea breeze, the constancy of the waves. They settle him after an overnight job. The momentary rest feels timeless. Beside him the statue of the mayor reads his newspaper forever. In the early hours of the morning, this companionable sitting together is fixed. Sometimes he dozes, leaning against the reading man, until the first metro aide comes sweeping by. But now the cold bronze makes him shiver.

He could not shoot that Jesus. That Jesus knew too much, staring at him like that, seeing him weep.

The toy revolver presses against his hip, mocking him. He remembers the folk ditty *Leron-Leron Sinta,* a silly love song.

> *Ako'y ibigin mo, lalaking matapang*
> *Hindi natatakot sa baril-barilan*
> *Ang sundang ko'y pito, ang baril ko'y siyam*
> *Isang pinggang pansit ang aking kalaban.*

> *Love me, a brave man*
> *Unafraid of playing shoot-outs*
> *My knives are seven, my guns nine*
> *A plate of noodles is my enemy.*

He shuts the knife. A crisp, urgent snap. He likes it—it's real.

After he left the church, he walked to the old malls. They were closed by then. He hung around the car parks. He didn't have to wait too long. Soon a man approached. He was much younger than the others and friendly in an ordinary way. He looked concerned about the boy's bruises. Elvis thought he was Filipino but he couldn't speak the language, or English. They went to a noodle house, quietly had a bowl each. They went to the toilets. It was quick, easy, no go-betweens. No more five-star arrangements, no lanterns as ploys, no games. He tells himself he likes this better. It's real and his own call. Like the next one at the car park. That was even quicker, though cheaper. The man was local so he bargained well.

<h2 style="text-align:center">85</h2>

"What's this, a wake?" a lantern seller asks.

"Worse," another murmurs. "Like some ginger tea?"

At a stall in the intersection, no one has slept. Yes, there's some relief because the bulldozer is gone, but still everyone wants to keep watch lest the police pick up anyone else. After the arrest they did stall to stall then house to house chats. They were after the men, especially all the male children. They hammered the hut shut and taped it with a sign: "Keep Out." Two police cars are parked nearby, and the traffic is still being rerouted. It's unnaturally quiet here where bonds are being repaired.

"I've got something stronger—like some?" Mang Gusting offers.

"Saint Michael, preserve us." Mang Pedring takes a swig.

Ginebra San Miguel. Reliable firewater in times like this. Even the women take turns.

"What misfortune," Lisa sighs, the fire in her throat and chest not quite a comfort.

"What do you think will happen?" Vic can't hide his worry, but still he works with meticulous care. Each piece of shell is polished, each held against the light to check for cracks. Everyone wonders why he doesn't stop, but no one has the heart to query his earnest labor. His brother is absent from this gathering. He took his time before he joined in, getting Vim drunk first so he'd sleep, so he'd stop blabbering about the cold steel on his skin, how he thought—he thought—

"I think you should tell your brother to shut up from now on. Don't get involved," Mario lectures him. "To save his neck, you know what I mean?"

"It's bad-luck Christmas for all of us." Manang Betya wrings her hands. "But we can shift luck...we'll figure it out...." But her voice has no conviction and her numbers will never win. Here the odds are greater than the number of stars in the sky.

"Who would ever think that Nena and Noland, plus another boy, they say—ay, it's too much to think about." Lisa shakes her head sorrowfully. She has her own sorrows. She's been trying to catch the eye of Mang Gusting again, with little success. All these fears hanging around have made her even lonelier. "Noland. Of all people."

"You believe it?"

"Well, they found the Amerkana in there—"

"But a child, and a mute one at that—"

"A child *and* his mother. Don't forget they're together in this."

"I'm glad that Cate was found, otherwise—a war at our doorstep."

"We'd have lost everything."

Saint Michael has passed from hand to hand again; the bottle is empty.

"Bad-luck Christmas for all of us, except Mario, of course. So when did Helen find out, really?"

"She's probably the only one sound asleep now, with all that reward."

"How much did she get?"

"You're rich, Mario."

Mario waves all the remarks away, saying they haven't received anything, that it was probably just talk, and if they do, they'll give a big party and everyone will be invited. How's that?

Mang Gusting absentmindedly balances the empty bottle on an unfinished lantern, with no success. It topples down. Bad-luck Christmas. His thoughts have flown away to where someone hasn't sent a Christmas card. "What you see isn't always the true story," he murmurs to no one.

"Of course, how sure are we it's those kids? What about that Pizza Hut man?"

"That *terorista*?"

"No, it's *kultong terorista* now, didn't you know?" A terrorist cult, which leaves the others open-mouthed.

"You don't watch the news, but I do. That mother and son are probably part of a cult—"

"Ay, *Dios ko*, it's the devil among us."

"How terrible. Thank God they were taken away."

"They're not really from here, though, are they?"

"Yes, they've always kept to themselves, they're strangers."

The excision is swift and comforting. They're not one of us.

86

"It's cooler here in the early hours," the American journalist notes and Eugene agrees. He shivers. They haven't left their post outside the police compound. The media have dwindled but a curious crowd of vagrants trickle by. A rice-cake wheelie stall is parked among them. The enterprising vendor has instant coffee and ginger tea on the side. The crowd is fed and warmed.

"How can they do this to a child?"

"You mean, how can a child do this?"

"I don't believe that."

"What don't you believe? Cate Burns was found in his hut."

"And that means an abduction and the child's a terrorist—you kidding?"

"A terrorist conspiring with that Pizza Hut man in

whom the police seem to have lost interest now. Don't forget, the first case and the real one is the murder of one of us."

"And the terrorist cult?"

"You're pursuing the American conspiracy line."

"I pursue every line in my job."

The conjectures usher in the day, and the casual rounds of the police to keep the small crowd from the gate. They'll all go home soon. It's Christmas Eve. The lanterns around the block flash a reminder.

"You really think it's an Abu Sayyaf cell?"

"Don't be stupid, the boy's Catholic."

"Who says?"

"Catholic or Muslim—what's the difference?"

"What a stupid question."

"What's stupid is if you don't ask that question. There are good and bad Catholics, or Christians if you will, and there are good and bad Muslims. There's violence and kindness on both sides, on any side—it's just people."

"What do you mean, it's just people? You're a fence sitter."

"At least I have a better view from here, and I'm not saying it makes me any better. I'm as good and bad as everyone else, but I wish I were better—"

"Better at what—arguments in your newspaper column?"

"I wish—I wish we could invent a compassion drug, inject politicians with it and all those who hold the lives of the most powerless—"

Someone laughs. "You making some corny speech?"

"No, just wishing for an antidote against unscrupulous self-interest."

The laughing man sobers up. "A drug for decency is enough for me."

"Then in this case, we're dreaming." Another closes the subject and walks away. "I'm going home."

The wishes are hushed, as they are around the world where the stars want to hide their faces, afraid to be picked on by another futile human longing. The small crowd of journalists and cameramen look away from each other. All know there's little chance for the boy and his mother in there, but no one can bear to say it.

"We must be vigilant, anything can happen now."

"Everything has happened—we should be doing something more than hanging around for the next tidbit."

A cameraman starts texting again. "I've been asking friends to come. We should all go to the streets and protest—"

"At Christmas?"

A policeman and a photographer buy rice cakes and ginger tea. A vagrant who's looking on gets a cake from the policeman. The photographer throws in a tea. All nod to each other as they take their first bite.

"If Germinio were alive, he'd be in there giving them a headache."

"That's why he's not alive."

Eugene envies the others who haven't stopped arguing through the night, but he's past talking. The story is over. There are culprits in custody, so everyone is appeased. Everyone will go home and have Christmas. He's ashamed of his thoughts, but his exhaustion overwhelms his shame. He hasn't slept in his own bed since the shooting, but he can't bring himself to leave.

"They'll use children to exonerate murderers."

"We won't let that happen. That's why we're here."

And you believe that. Eugene shivers. It's colder than he thought.

87

At 6 a.m. the waiting room is unlocked and some weak coffee and *pan de sal* are brought in. Mother and son don't move, still bound together like one body, curled against the wall. The couch hasn't been used. All night they listened to the screaming in the cell at the other end, the passing footsteps, and each little sound behind the door. Nena was certain it would open anytime and they'd be wrenched apart, and this time she might never see her son again. She tried to imagine the farm when there were still the three of them listening to the first crickets, watching the stars rise from the hill.

Sometime in the night she whispered the old story-wish to her son. The stars above the hill are angels and they're watching over us. Noland saw the hill but there were no stars. It was broad daylight and very hot. Heat waves rose from the rice that looked almost white at high noon. Nena felt his sweat trickle on her breast and thighs, but she did not ease her clasp and nor did he. Not even air must be allowed to come between them. She only moved her lips, intoning the wish as before:

Star-light, star-bright
Make-a-wish-a-wish-tonight.

But Noland saw no stars to wish on. He'd lost all of them in his head. Even the comic strip has gone.

"It's breakfast," the guard says, pushing the tray closer to the prisoners. It bothers him that they're still in the same position as when he locked the door last night. "It's breakfast," he says again, still hoping to see their faces.

88

He's drawn into the little boxes, the little angels falling and flying. Here's one with a drooping wing, here's another with a startled look on her face, another with stick-hands raised in the air. He wants to know what happens next but it seems the same story is told in pages and pages of comic strips strung together. Roberto Espinosa flips through the notebook and finds the large star with the photos pasted on it, the mandala identified by someone stupid enough to pronounce it a cultic symbol. The boy's a lantern maker and this is a sketch of a lantern. Why can't they see that? Because of the photos, one of the farmer who murdered his landlord six years ago in what was alleged to be a ritual killing. Because of the yet unpasted photo: the American.

This circus is making him sick but he's part of it and there's no way out. That little act with the Americans at the hospital was the worst yet. And now, this. So who started the rumor about a terrorist cult? It began in that hut, an offhand remark overheard by the media, and now the public laps it up. It's a wonder how a story is told and retold in a matter of hours. How it lands on his desk as "truth."

Roberto takes his first coffee on what will be a very long day. The phone rings. Finally he takes the call that he's tried to avoid all night.

89

The consul has breakfast at her desk. The colonel is angling for a quarrel. A man going around the bend is the last thing she needs after the phone hasn't stopped ringing all night.

"Let me speak with the ambassador."

"For God's sake, drop it, David." Her cup clunks on the saucer, spilling coffee. She almost curses. "We must distance ourselves from this case."

"Because we got back our own?"

She's trying to find the napkin. "It's impolitic—now where's that—it's impolitic to keep stirring—"

"Like hell we stirred it up! All that spin. So why can't we tell one more story, the truth this time?"

"Truth?" She blots the spill with letterhead paper. "C'mon, you're tired, I'm tired." Her voice cajoles as though he's a peeved child. "It's not the time to debate truth, David."

"Aw, don't give me that, Bettina. All I'm asking is for us to make a statement based on Cate's claim that the mother and son are innocent—is that too onerous a task? If we can mobilize the demolition of hundreds of lives—"

"Wait a minute, that wasn't us, that was a local strategy. Besides, it didn't happen, it wasn't meant to happen, and afterward we got results anyway. Someone reported the culprits—but of course you think they're innocent. My God, David, the father was a murderer!"

"Have you asked why?"

The consul is flabbergasted. "Where's your loyalty? Doesn't it bother you that this is another hostage crisis involving an American citizen? You of all people should understand the implication of this case. Hasn't it occurred to you that the Abu Sayyaf have grown so bold as to take action in the heart of the capital—at the busiest time of the year? Terrorists in this country are linked to bombings in other parts of the world, and then those assassinations, kidnappings, the beheadings—have you gone blind?"

David hears the string of arguments in his head. What if we're wrong? What if this "terrorist group" is nothing more than a gang of kidnappers used to discredit the Muslim guerilla armies that have fought for self-determination since the seventies? Where does the story begin? Have we asked about the years of dispossession of Mindanao's Muslims? Do we *know* this country? Have we asked about the endemic corruption of this government, the violence of its military against civilians, and the even greater violence of poverty? Have we asked why that farmer hacked his landlord to death? But we're not allowed to go there. We stick with the present where the storytelling is required to begin, where we should always tell "the truth" with certainty.

"So, Bettina, you really believe that this case with the boys is a hostage crisis?"

"And what do you believe, David? You went to Afghanistan, Iraq—what do you believe in?"

Afghanistan he believed in: he had no love for the Taliban. Then Iraq. He believed in that too, oh how he believed in those weapons of mass destruction, and then? Certainty is terrifying. Whoever wields it.

He keeps his anger at bay. "A kid, a lantern seller, is an Abu Sayyaf operative in the slums of Manila, is that it?"

"What do you think?"

He laughs, bitterly. "A Hollywood conspiracy. C'mon, the boy's hut is filled with stars and angels. He's Catholic.

It's not Allah, Bettina, it's a different God. But the spin doctors left that out, of course."

"God's on our side, so we got back our own."

He can't believe his ears. He finds himself shaking. "Allah, Christ—who cares? Whatever god it is, we use him as a badge for our possession or dispossession. We justify or we implore, and then we start a fucking war!"

She's unflustered, keeping up the solemn tone. "Of course you know the Burnses have an uncle who's high up at the Pentagon."

He ignores the remark.

"Of course you know. That's probably why you've been asked to handle the case. The family pulled strings and they thought they could trust the people's colonel—and what other secret designations do you have, David? Are you CIA, or simply Pentagon?" She shrugs at his lack of response. "I wonder what they'd say if they heard you now."

He refuses to take the bait.

"I'm going to keep my mouth shut about this conversation, but for the moment let's just do our job. Self-righteousness is not part of our brief." Then she tries to make peace. "Another coffee?"

David shakes his head. She pours herself a third cup. "Well, the Philippine media hounded us all last night—at least you don't have to deal with that. They're demanding we save the children and produce Cate as a witness against The Pizza Hut Man." She chuckles.

"Yes, as thick as a Hollywood plot." But her amusement is brief. "We're flying her home."

He remains silent. What's the use?

"You know what they're saying? Cate Burns must appease a restless public. She's a witness to a crime that's become very difficult for the Philippine government. And why should their children be put in the firing line? It's the responsibility of America, as a friend, to help. Whose friend are you, David?"

Overnight, since the arrest, the embassy has issued a statement: Cate Burns is in intensive care and the U.S. won't undermine the Philippine government's very competent handling of the case. Not too cool or abrupt but efficiently shutting up the protest at the other end. There's the necessary rift between truth and diplomatic truth.

The consul walks to the window, raises her cup to the stars hanging from the acacia trees, all festive above the U.S. marines milling about and, outside the gate, the armored cars of the Philippine military. "There's talk about a protest rally if the embassy doesn't hand her over. A threat of people power in this street, but we're used to it and all that 'Down with the imperialist' stuff. We can't win, can we? Around the world if there's trouble, they seek our help; if we help, they accuse us of meddling. What are we supposed to do?"

David wants to gag her, but his shaking hands find only his face, which no longer feels like his own.

"You know what really gets me? It's the fact that

we liberated this country from the Japanese. Your grandfather fought for that, or have you forgotten? We gave them democracy, an educational system, we still feed them foreign aid, and what do we get in return?"

David hears the equal bitterness of the Filipina journalist on the television panel. After a while, he whispers tiredly, "Forty years, Bettina. We occupied them for forty years, and before that, we fought them in a war, and much later, we backed the dictator who robbed them blind for twenty years."

But she barely hears. She's searching the streets for any sign of activity. "Yes, possibly people power again. But this is a country that performs its protest, and performances can be exhausting. One must draw the curtain sometimes for rest—the restless public must have their Christmas too."

"Are you done, Bettina?"

"Go home, David…it's Christmas Eve." She leads the silent man to the door, convinced that her ambassador must ring Washington. This new military attaché, or whatever is his undocumented designation, has lost the plot. Whoever posted him here has made a dangerous mistake.

90

He likes his fried rice with plenty of garlic, and his dried fish salty and crisp. Senator G.B. is having "a poor man's breakfast," but only rarely—it's not healthy, you know. This is what he confides on the phone after inquiring about the detainees and how the search for the other boy is progressing. Offhand, he suggests that they must be moved somewhere safe from the media. All this drumbeating about the poor child in custody might cause Roberto Espinosa to lose his job by the New Year. You know, *this* could hurt any career irreparably, but he can speak to friends who will make sure this doesn't happen. But first, please take care of the situation. We don't want that cult messing up our turf, do we?

Senator G.B. likes his circuitous persuasions. He can speak to friends who will make sure someone loses his job if this isn't handled his way. He likes the stunned silence at the other end as this point is digested. He likes breakfast with a little kick on the side, to start the day. "And Roberto, thanks for accommodating our American friend, we'll talk again soon."

He splashes whisky into his coffee and turns the television on. Thank God he has his own media. If the mother and son disappear tonight, there might be a story about another abduction by the cult. A tale is only as fresh as its fodder.

"Honey, are you still making those phone calls?"

"Ah, Margarita, *mi amor*, come here—I don't know

what I'd have done without you over these last few days." He kisses his wife, who is twenty years his junior. He married her when she was an upcoming singer and shifted her career toward singing for his religious charities, which earned him the nickname Good Boy.

"Really, G.B., Jingjing's been waiting to have breakfast with her dad for an hour now. It's getting too much, you know, we've got to put a stop to this. Can we at least eat at the table like family?" She picks up his coffee and confiscates the little flask, slipping it into her pocket.

"Just a minute." He flips channels, then stops. "Again?" He's furious. "How many times do they have to show that? *Putang ina*!" he curses the TV. "If there's any more tugging at the heartstrings, they'll snap."

The camera is meticulously panning across the boy's face as if it were the most precious find. It lingers on the eyes that outstare the lens.

91

Is it a downward turn of the mouth or a crease on the brow? Or a wariness in the eyes? Something else is there, or something is missing. She can't find what has made his face strange, or what it has lost.

Nena urges her son to eat. He stares up at her, also querying her face, then burrows deep into her breast again. Does she know?

She dare not ask now, she dare not find out. "If they ask, we know nothing," she whispers.

She thought it out through the night. Today the uniforms will ask questions, will ask for stories. About the American, the Pizza Hut man, about that bad-luck woman, about things she can't even ask her son after he went missing. She rehearses denials in her head—but about what? What did she or her son *not* do? Her breath quickens, quick as the little mice in her legs, scurrying, gnawing. Once in a circle of uniforms she was asked questions about her husband, about the altar on their wall and the pictures of their dead ancestors beside the crucifix, about the missing machete, about who their friends were and how long they'd hated the big house.

Never, in all her life, has she been asked what has been done to her family. Her back aches, her limbs are cramped, but she can't disengage herself from her son. Sometime in the night she needed to go to the toilet but she was terrified to talk to the guard outside. She longed to stretch out, tried to crawl to the couch with Noland in her arms, but he whimpered piteously. She whispered the story about the stars on the hill. He grew quiet and fell asleep.

92

This story began with a star. At the airport she imagined it flashed a warning. Two hours later it seduced her out of a taxi and spun her life out of her hands. Cate peers at it through drugged eyes. The patchwork of shells at the window is still, unlit. Her life and other lives once so alien have all become a patchwork. Six accidental days and they're bound in one story.

She tries to rewind the tape in her head to before the flight, the taxi ride to the airport on the other side of the world, to a sleek apartment at leafy Cornell, the bedroom, the man in the bed who did not even know she was taking off to another country. She ran away with his smell still on her, the imprint of his unwelcome lovemaking in the early hours evoking the other welcome ones years ago, for this is how it happens when it's over. The final and the first act converge, and you see clearly.

He was her lecturer at Cornell. She was an impressionable freshman and she desired this gray-haired god and vowed to get him. They were married after her graduation and she desired more than just the scent of his spunk on her skin. She wanted it in her, growing, and he said to wait because he was finishing his third book, and then wait because he was setting up cutting-edge research with Oxford, and then wait because he was going for the professorial chair, and then wait some more, for what she doesn't even remember now.

Child evasion is like tax evasion, she once argued

with him. Cook up the books for debit, cry poor, or poor me, and wait for the taxman to validate your withdrawal from the ranks of fatherhood. It is this waiting that remains with her. Everything else has grown shadowy, like something under mossy water, so her eyes return to the surface, which becomes a screen playing six days as a lifetime, ending with an oh-so-solemn face in her head, with a kick in her womb.

She closes her eyes, opens them again. After days in that hut and the creek nearby, she drowns in this antiseptic smell, with a touch of flowers. She squints at the wall, so white now, as if someone has painted it afresh. No, not so white, but empty. The television is gone.

Yesterday when her visitors left, Cate thought she could ask someone, anyone, in the hospital for news. She opened the door. The two Americans stood up simultaneously, trying to look solicitous. "Anything you need, Cate?" She shook her head, shut the door again. She paced till midnight, pushing her panic down. From the window she saw a busy street dripping with fairy lights, figured her room was high up. She changed into street clothes, but what could she do? She lifted the phone. Who does she know in this city? She turned on the television, and laughed at her last resort. How absurd: when in trouble, watch TV. But surely there will be news about her rescue, about *them*.

The programs were mostly Christmas extravaganzas she couldn't understand. She flipped channels and found CNN. She stopped, distracted, not by the news but by the inflections of home in the voice of the anchorwoman. Always an easy confidence, even in stories of disaster. Iraq filled the screen, then the usual honor roll of dead American soldiers, naming each one, validating a life, its loss, the stars and stripes ever present in the picture. Those grim and somber stars.

Then the rhetoric on the war against terrorism, still calm, directed against another part of the globe. She could hardly breathe as she came face to face with herself: Cate Burns rescued from a terrorist cult in the Philippines! The Abu Sayyaf now has its claws into the capital. This hostage crisis is more chilling than the earlier cases in Mindanao, because of its "bizarre circumstances." Then the clip of the helicopter over the lantern stalls, the railway track, the huts, and Nena and Noland as she had last seen them, while the anchorwoman asked, "Can a child be part of a terrorist conspiracy?"

"How—I—" Cate felt she'd be sick. She burst into the adjoining lounge, heading for the door, but was detained by the guards.

"Can we help?"

"I've got to go to them—they're innocent—"

"Innocent?" One of the men led her from the door. "What do you mean?"

"Nena and Noland, the mother and her son—"

"I'm sure they're okay. Now go back to bed. Everything will be fine."

"Don't patronize me!" she snapped. "I saw them on TV. They said they're terrorists—how—I must go, they're innocent, I know it, we've got to help them, please, I've got to go." She began to struggle.

"Sorry, we can't allow—"

"Can't allow what—innocence?" She hit the arm detaining her. "Of course you're supposed to be guarding it."

One man kept leading her back to her room, but the other guard couldn't restrain his impatience. "Let's get this clear. The case is a local matter and you're an American citizen."

"What's it got to do with being American?"

"Everything." The man was shocked that this screaming woman had missed the point. "The last thing we need is a hysterical—"

She slapped him. "Don't you even fucking care?" Then she kept screaming, hitting at the men dragging her back inside, and the doctor walked in and all went hazy, save for the grim and somber stars.

93

The widow watches the morning news as she sorts the boxes: what will be used for the case, what will be kept, what will be given away. Last night, she packed all her husband's possessions—mostly files, papers and more papers, and only two boxes of clothes. Her Jimmy never cared about what he wore. His colors clashed; he thought darning socks was a waste of time. He cared only about his stories and the arguments that went on forever in his head. She could hear him thinking while they made love. Once he mumbled something about an extra-judicial killing, perhaps a line for a story. It infuriated her. His sense of justice was more ardent than his desire. She pushed him away and he murmured, "How can I love you if I don't love what makes us human?"

The news plays again the clip of the mother screaming as she's wrenched away from her boy.

What makes us human? That mother's despair, its resonance in my gut. The widow hears herself answering the dead.

The news confirms that the boy was there when her husband was shot. So was an older boy, a street kid, who hasn't been found, not yet, but they've identified him now.

Again and again her hands sweep back her hair, and her eyes gather the room. *What makes us human* — can she ever sweep this back into place?

The boys sold lanterns together. The mute boy sold her husband a lantern just before the shooting. Was this, in fact, a sign for the assassin? In the boy's hut, they found blood on his lanterns, possibly the American's. The investigation continues.

She sighs at the screen. That we can fabricate stories is what makes us human and keeps us at the top of the food chain.

Again the speculation about a terrorist cult, but less

incredulous than in last night's broadcast. And if indeed this cult exists, what happens to the allegations against Senator G.B.? There's a quick clip of the senator having breakfast with his family. He pours his daughter a glass of milk, he kisses his young wife.

What makes us human? The widow feels sick to her stomach. She wants to argue with the dead.

94

Almost everyone knows about the other boy by now, except the boy himself. He's asleep beside the mayor reading a paper. A metro aide shakes him awake. It's midday at the Baywalk. The tourist strip must not be littered by vagrants, at least not this bench.

"Not here, boy." The metro aide keeps shaking him.

Elvis stares at the tinsel strand hanging over the man's shirt with the picture of the country's president. "W-what?" He's disoriented.

"Sleep wherever, just not here." The man waves him away.

"You want to sweep me up too?" Elvis is quickly himself again.

"Be grateful it's me, not the police. By the way, what happened to that eye, huh?"

"I'm awake now, so why heckle me? The police have nothing against enjoying the sea breeze—do you?"

"I'm just being helpful," the metro aide says grudgingly, and gets on with the sweeping.

"Asshole!" the boy calls out to him in English and feels almost all right again. He pats the gun at his hip, then the knife, runs a hand over his bruises, and buttons up his shirt. The last time he washed was with that tourist who roughed him up in the shower. He grooms himself, wetting his hair with a bit of spit, pulling his collar just so to hide the rip, then puts on his cap, turning it this way and that for the right angle. He takes time with these details, slowly collecting himself, but try as he might there's a piece that he can't retrieve. He'll never know what happened in the room next to his in that hotel. Maybe it was really just pictures. But Bobby is a liar.

The sea breeze is a mercy. Christmas Eve is promising to be even hotter and the traffic is hopeless. The last minute shopping, the rushed homecomings and the revelries buzz around the boy gathering the remains of himself.

95

The man who walks in is not in uniform. He's gray and small; he looks like someone's grandfather. Nena is relieved. And he has a tray of rice and hot chicken soup, and Coke and sweet peanut cakes. Behind him, the guard is carrying a table for the lunch and thinking that the prisoners have better fare than he does. He sniffs the air; he can smell pee. He begins to say something but the chief frowns to silence him, shows him where to set the table, then sends him off.

"So Nena and Noland, shall we have lunch? By the way, I'm Roberto. I help around here." He notes that the breakfast is untouched. "I'm hungry, come." He begins setting out the dishes.

Nena shifts on the floor; the boy whimpers.

"Are you hungry too, Noland?" he asks.

"Please, sir, he can't speak and he doesn't—and we don't know anything, sir."

"I know—but call me Mang Bert. And let's eat."

"My son, he's not well—"

"So he must eat."

The mother whispers into her son's ear. He whimpers in response. They're still locked together, trying to look small.

When the senator rang, Roberto felt more anger than dread. He could hardly speak. When he walked in just now, he felt it again. Terrorist cult? Look at them now, cowering against that wall. But he had to smile, had to be nice. He made sure he ordered a good lunch. While waiting, he went over the boy's angels again, all the winged stick figures, then the phone rang for the nth time: "Move the prisoners away from the media. They're all out to get me, so do what you can and if you don't—"

The chief makes sure he does this alone. He will make it as painless as possible. He will try.

"It's yummy chicken soup, Noland." He takes it to the boy, close enough to whet his appetite.

The mother receives the soup. She takes a spoonful. "Have a bit, Noland, you haven't eaten anything since yesterday." Since you came home, she wants to say. "Just a sip." She can't say more.

I sipped so much of the red stuff back there and fell asleep for a long time. Noland remembers but he can't tell his mother, who turns his face away from her chest so he can have a sip.

"You say he's unwell."

She nods as she forces some soup into her son's mouth.

"What happened, Nena?"

She keeps feeding the boy soup. It runs down his chest.

"Did anyone hurt you, Noland?"

She is crying. It's good to be asked, ay, it's good to be asked.

96

The wheelie stall has ditched rice cakes and tea for proper lunch. It disappeared for a while, then returned with a pot of rice, fried fish, and mung bean soup. The vendor even brought a bench for his customers, and his nine-year-old daughter. She's quick on her feet, used to this kind of work. Only three media people have remained but there's still talk about possible people power. Business could be good yet.

People power is hope performed. Thank God for the big, fervid show. A dictator, a corrupt president is overthrown. A dam is arrested, a mine, the rape of a forest, the powerful machine churning against us. Masses take to the streets to unhinge the world from its axis. Here's hoping.

A cameraman texts another activist friend. "I'm sure she'll come, I'm sure they'll all come. One more rice, please," he tells the girl.

He works with Eugene, who wants to snap back, get real! Aren't you tired of people power? These days it's more of a mob desperate to get a few pesos, a free lunch, and a T-shirt from whoever is organizing a cause. Years ago, we marched and died on the streets. Now we die in ourselves, in our fear or sheer exhaustion. Or simply indifference, the safest of all.

But Eugene is afraid to speak. He keeps his head down over his meal. The boss in the studio has been ringing them to make sure they return the gear. Not enough cameras to cover Christmas Eve and anyway Eugene should be at the wedding of a politician's daughter and a shipping tycoon. It's the wedding of the year, a Christmas tying of the knot by two of the most powerful Filipino families. Why aren't they answering calls? Because they're on a stakeout outside the police station, not so much for a story but for hope, which left, piece by piece, as the media went home. See you, call me if anything happens. The barricade is dismantled, the police return inside the gate, or perhaps home.

As Eugene picks the bones from his fish, he thinks of his mother, he thinks of the sea in his village. Wouldn't it be nice... He's ashamed of them all, their wish for rest, their resignation.

"Hoy, Eugene, she's coming after all," the cameraman waves his phone around as if blessing his mung bean soup. The phone beeps: another message. "And that American who left this morning, he says he'll come back later and we'll get that boy out. Oh yes, they'll all come back."

Eugene is dying to sleep in his own bed.

97

"Did they hurt your friend too?" He speaks slowly, full of sympathy. He spoons more rice onto the boy's plate. He's sitting with him now on the couch, and eating. The boy is ravenous.

"He's not a friend, sir, he's bad-bad, a devil boy," the mother protests.

"Really? And why's that?"

The mother ignores the question, afraid she's said too much.

"He could be hungry, too, Noland, wherever he is."

The boy remembers twelve fish-ball sticks for the twelve days of Christmas, and the noodles at midnight, the McDonald's pancakes with sweet water on them, and the full revolution of a cap when the tummy is full and warm.

"Where do you think is he, Noland?"

He doesn't want to remember more.

"Don't you think we should find out if he's okay?"

"That whore-child," the mother says through gritted teeth. The thought cuts through her breast.

"What was that, Nena?"

She stops eating; she has lost all appetite. She puts an arm around her son, pulling him away from the strange man who is trying to be kind. "Can we go home now, sir?"

"Ah . . . maybe we can go to another home, somewhere secret and safe. Those who hurt your son might return to the hut, who knows."

"Ay, yes sir. Thank you sir, thank you." She grabs his hand and kisses it.

The chief feels an uneasy flush in his chest. But he smiles and allows the woman to lap up his benevolence.

98

By late afternoon Elvis is back with the mayor reading his newspaper, an empty McDonald's bag between them as if they've just had a snack together. Earlier he wandered off to the old red-light district, trying his luck, but everyone seemed to be rushing off somewhere, frantic in their revelry, strides purposeful, bags of gifts secure, stomachs primed for the midnight Christmas feast in a few hours. No time for chance adventures. Even the secret brothel behind a moneychanger's shop was closed.

Elvis huddles close to the mayor. It used to be perfect here, before they added this other man pointing out to sea. The statue of the murdered senator makes the boy uneasy. It's as if he knows that something's out there and he's not telling Elvis. He's looking far away, unaware that Elvis exists. But the mayor, he's different. He lends him an arm when he's tired. In another life, perhaps he would ask him, "What are you reading?" And the mayor would hush him like a proper father and tell him to go and play.

What are you reading? Elvis has no clue that, around the city, many have read about him, the other boy, including Bobby Cool.

In an old apartment above a row of shops, Bobby is waking up with a hangover, and reading the afternoon tabloid makes his head throb even more. He's like a proper father in his initial shock. My God, where's that boy now? So *it* all happened under his very nose. Ah, those sneaky boys made a fool out of him. Then the possibilities unfold. The pimp sees himself saving the boy all over again, the two of them running away from the big city to start anew perhaps in an island resort with all those happy, spending tourists. He could retire from wheeling and dealing through the smog.

It never lifts, not in this part of the city. Over Manila Bay the smog is perpetual; one barely sees the blue sky, but Elvis never looks for it. He cases the passersby, intent on the foreign men, checking for clues. Who to approach, how to approach. He longs to be taken to a hotel, a bed, a shower. Maybe some lonely father-uncle-friend will take him in till Christmas. Once Bobby arranged such a man for him. The Austrian took him to a resort. He took in another boy from the local village. They swam and partied for two days. He taught them Christmas carols in his language. He was the nicest ever.

99

Night has fallen. There are more monsters in the shadows and trust is harder to muster. David is stopped at the gate.

"Sorry, the chief isn't here. The boy and his mother aren't here. Do you have an ID, sir? Can we see it, please? Sorry, we can't let you in." The guard looks him over suspiciously.

He tries to be nice, he argues, but knows it's futile. After the meeting with the consul he drove around, willingly got stranded by traffic, shopped for his daughters, and thought some more. Should he return to the hospital? But what could he say? Should he go home? "Go home, David, Come home, David." Everyone is sending him home, that vulnerable place which justifies arsenals, the reason invoked when we go to war. We must protect *our* home; everyone against *our* home is evil; there's no other home outside *ours*. He's been going home forever. The long journey is a wretched pilgrimage. It does a man in. He can't return, because he can't leave what he has become. These days his wife despises him, he's sure of it; she flinches when he comes close. But his little daughters love him desperately, or maybe it's the other way round. He's afraid for them, for all those children he's seen. He wonders what his grandfather would have said. Surely he would have commiserated with him—he understood war. Or did he? Once as a frail old man, he showed his grandson his medals. David remembers hugging him. Then he heard him whisper, "It's not patriotism that wins you these, boy...not what keeps you fighting in the thick of it...but because there's nothing else to do, and you're so damned afraid the other guy will shoot first." Then he felt a hand patting his back, a tremulous assurance. "Sometimes...I'm ashamed."

"Sir—sir, did you hear what I said?"

"Yes?" David realizes the guard has been trying to explain something to him. "I said, I'm looking for Roberto Espinosa—he knows me, Colonel David Lane. I'm here about the boy and his mother."

"Sorry, sir, but I told you they're not here and the chief went home, it's Christmas Eve, you know."

The guard's tone is softly humoring, as if talking to a child. Or maybe he has read the memories in the American's face. David turns away. Across the road, a small crowd has gathered. One man is holding up a placard: "Free Noland and Nena!" He returns to his car. Around the compound the star lanterns light up, and the Christmas tree.

100

"When do we go, sir?"

"Soon, Nena, soon—but tell me, how long have you lived in Manila?"

"A long time, sir."

"Just with your son?"

The mother nods. "My son's a good boy. He makes good lanterns."

Noland is crouched behind her. He can't return to her lap, because the man will look him in the eye. His arms are around her waist, his face in the hollow of her back. She smells as she did on a hot day working on the farm, and something else, like his own smell when he wets his pants. It makes him feel ashamed for her, before this man who's sitting so close.

"So we'll go very soon, sir?"

The chief touches her arm sympathetically. "I know it's hard to raise a boy on your own. You must miss his father."

The mother wrings her hands—"No, no, sir"—clasps them, pleading, "I mean, don't say—"

"He was a farmer, right?"

"Please, please don't say any more, sir." She rubs the boy's back, hushing him before it starts. For years, she has told stories about the hill, the stars there, the angels, but never uttering the name that long ago drove the boy whimpering to the wall for days. Her stories have remained suspended in the night sky, never descending onto that hill.

"You must miss him too, Noland."

"No, please—"

"I mean, your friend—what's his name? He sold lanterns with you, didn't he?"

"Elvis, he's called Elvis, and he's not his friend," Nena is quick to reply, ready to talk about the other boy now. What can she say, what does she know? "He's bad, a devil boy, he—he—" But she knows nothing more. "Are we going now, sir?"

She feels the head thumping her back.

"Is that true, Noland, your friend's a devil?"

The hand is clawing her waist.

"And he was with you when the Pizza Hut man came?"

"He has nothing to do with that—that—"

"And he hurt your friend, didn't he? The Amerkana.

But you saved her. You took her to your hut and took care of her. That was very brave, Noland."

The angel, the angel, he hears himself say, but no one hears.

101

There is no angel. The field is white. The sweat trickles on the back of his knees as he sits at the door. The white rises up to a hill. He hears his mother muttering, "It's so hot, it's so hot," then more words, like she's praying.

"It's so hot, Noland, but we're not staying. You heard what the man said? We'll be somewhere safe and secret soon, and you've been very brave."

The mother and son are alone again in the waiting room, but Noland is elsewhere now. He's back in the hut, waiting at the door, and his mother is waiting too with her dense murmurings that make him afraid. No matter. He will sit at the door, even if there's no angel yet.

"It's going to be all right, we'll be out of here before Christmas. But we have to tell the man where that monster is. So where does Elvis hang out? Hoy, are you listening?"

The rice is a shimmering white field at noon. When the sun sets it will turn to gold. The mother clutches her four-year-old to her breast; the urgency makes him more afraid. He escapes her arms, returns to the door to wait.

"Are you listening, Noland? That Elvis is no friend of

yours, and we'll stick to that story whoever asks. Re-member that, *whoever asks.* He's a street kid making trou-ble, making bad-bad trouble, you understand?"

102

Ah, these stick figures sprouting wings. Roberto Es-pinosa is sidetracked again. His hands shake as he scans the notebook. It's lack of sleep since the shooting—when was that? Five, six days ago, but it seems years away. He's feeling his age, afraid the case will wreck his retirement. He orders a car to take all the captives to a safe house, that is, when we find the other boy—no, we haven't found him yet, Senator. The man was swearing when he put the phone down. His sixth call of the day.

He returns to the mandala. He studies each photo at each point of the star. The father and mother are young smiling photos. The mute boy between them is sad and serious, eyes veered to the right as if trailing some pro-found thought. The picture of the other boy is from a photo booth. The cap angled to the side shadows a pug-nacious look. He dares the chief to drop his eyes first.

This photo was published in the afternoon papers. The police are out in full force now, scouring the usual places: the shady hotels, the karaoke bars, the malls, the shad-owy parks. The mother didn't say it, nor did she give a name, but Roberto understood the story of the devil boy.

Who knows? Maybe it was a botched hold-up, a con job that grew into a hostage situation. Instigated by *this*. He thumps the photo of the other boy with his finger. Looks like he's capable of anything. Seduced the American with the lanterns and implicated the mute boy, and it was all going well until they thought she was shot, so they spirited her home. Was it panicked conscience—do children have that?—or a crazy adventure, even a dare?

He goes back to the tabloid clipping. The family was evicted from the hacienda that was to be subdivided, to prevent them from making their land claim. They'd farmed that land for generations, but only as "squatting" tenants, and then suddenly the landlord made other plans. So the father flipped. It happens, it happened. All for land, violent land. But where did the story begin, the bloodletting?

The media will feast on the boy's history when it gets out, so let's deal with the present. Humor the senator, hide the witnesses against his hired hit man or turn them into culprits—of course, everyone is innocent unless proven guilty. Ah, there's blood on all our hands. He studies the photos of the boys again, trapped in a star. Yes, save the senator and save himself, his job, save everyone. A safe house then, safe from the news cannibals until the New Year, and maybe, just maybe—he mulls over possibilities, over the faces on the star. It must be the angels, for where else can this inspiration spring from? He wants to save one boy, at least the one he knows, but the older one makes him drop his eyes. He turns the air conditioning to high. It's grown too warm in here. He peers through the blue blinds. Across the road is a pathetic crowd of protesters. Thank God, it's Christmas.

Somewhere in the city, Bobby thinks this too as he combs the streets on foot. Surely the police can't be bothered with a boy on Christmas Eve, because they already have one in custody. But he's wrong. Plainclothes police are on an exhaustive city tour. They need results so they can go home tomorrow at the latest.

On his own tour of the usual places, the other boy gets lucky with a backpacker. He looks like a boy himself with his fresh face and blond curls. In the park they play cowboys with Elvis's toy gun, then move on. They have a game of pool in a joint that plays disco carols. Elvis feels his ears might burst with the thumping bass. They barely hear each other. He motions to the man that he wants to sleep, so maybe they can go somewhere else? He's blond, he speaks English — surely he has a hotel room.

The man orders soft drinks for both of them and chooses a corner table, the farthest corner. Elvis's heart sinks.

Under the table he guides the boy's hand. Occasionally he applauds a good shot, smiling at the pool players. He finishes before the game. He tucks a hundred pesos into the boy's pocket and leaves.

Cheap! In the toilet Elvis curses the hundred-peso bill. What an insult. When he sees that man again, he'll— He splashes his face, picks at the remains of soap on the sink and tries to make some lather. He doesn't look good. The bruises are still there and his clothes are a shame. That's why the blond man thought he was cheap. He turns his cap around, flap to the other side to change his luck.

103

There is no angel, but stars abound, almost stars. Fairy lights form a canopy over the street. It seems as if the giant banyans on each side have spread out for this purpose, extending their leafy arms toward each other, so the street can boast of a Milky Way as exclusive as the hospital. Here, the suites match those at five-star hotels, and everyone smiles at the American visitor—except in the private lounge where the two agents nod at him with a weary look.

David is briefed about the woman in the other room. The account sounds like a bored aside: last night she tried to leave the hospital, she was delusional, screaming, she had to be contained—and they had to take the TV out, the phone too. She's sleeping now. Will the colonel be staying long? One of the men starts to dial his phone. David puts up his hand and whispers, "No need. The embassy knows I'm here."

He waits, thinks of the right words, phrases them into an easier story in his head. The sleeping woman mumbles and swings out one arm, then the other, fending off something. Her mumbling grows more agitated, the syllables harsh, like little explosions in his ears.

"Cate . . . Cate," David whispers. "It's all right, Cate."

"All right?" she whispers back, tears in the corners of her eyes.

David holds the hand that has closed into a fist. "It's David from the embassy. It's all right, it's safe."

"Oh David. . . ."

"Yes. It's all right."

The tears well up as she whispers, "Did you ask for me?"

"Cate . . . your friends . . . they're in police custody, but I'll see what —"

She turns to the wall. "No one sees."

He wishes he hadn't come.

"Are you American?" she asks, sounding confused.

"Yes, of course," he assures her.

After a while, she murmurs, "What does it mean . . . what is it to be American?" The question stuns him. That he doesn't know how to answer stuns him more. Or maybe he doesn't know the answer. Maybe certainty is impossible. We're only as real as what we do and what is done to us in the moment; knowing comes much later, if it comes at all. We're jostled by too many acts that we choose to forget.

The woman turns to him again, pulling him to her. Into his ear she whispers, "What is it to be you . . . or me?" The questions are slowly strung together, as if some other thought keeps getting in the way.

"...Or a child?"

"I—I don't know." It's the most honest thing he has said in a long time.

104

The chief is taking his last chance. The notebook is still open at the clipping from six years ago. Maybe if he plays this wild card, the mother and son will cough up something new. Maybe he can get results before the day is over, and painlessly, he hopes.

The mute boy comes out of hiding. He traces the photo with a finger. The mother is almost in tears, mouthing, "No, no, please sir, no—not this." The pain in her legs is excruciating, ay, the little gnawing mice.

Two years ago, Noland found the photo under his mother's clothes. He thought it was a pretty picture of his mother and a little boy, and he wanted to paste it into his notebook. Nena remembers trying to grab it back before realizing that it was only the picture that made sense to him. Of course, her son can't read. She rode on his delight at the find, telling him this was little Noland long ago on the farm where the hill had stars that were angels who watched over them. He slept soundly that night, his head full of angels, but not one strayed into his mother's dream. She was on a desolate hill, keeping watch over the hut below, which was empty, and she kept wondering when everyone would come home.

"That's you, Noland, right?" The chief's voice is soft, kind.

Nena and little Noland. The boy looks and looks, then closes his eyes, draws the picture in his head, searching for the next scene, trying to return to his "secret" craft. Finally the faint scribbles, then the lines shaping up. Field. Hill. Sky. It's a strange comic strip trailing the tabloid box, and he's perplexed. He looks up at his mother, sees her distress, then studies the picture again.

"You remember that time, Noland?" The chief imagines history passing through the boy's face, those solemn eyes.

The mother turns her son around, her distress brusque, bruising. His arms hurt.

"Noland, we must tell this man where Elvis is, so we can go home." But he only stares. She shakes him. "He's not your friend, don't you understand? Why don't you ever listen to me? Why do you always get us into trouble?" But he keeps staring, trying to see the hill in her eyes. What was it like?

"You remember the farm, Noland?" the chief asks.

It was hot and the rice was white.

"My son and I, we didn't do anything, sir, and that was long ago—"

"You remember going up that hill, Noland?"

"Stop it—stop it, please—he didn't mean it, he didn't mean it." She begins to sob.

The chief takes the notebook from the boy, who

doesn't protest. In his head he sees that the hill has a little rise and sometimes the clouds hide it. But he saw it clearly from the door of the hut, like a little hill on a hill.

"How could you do this to us?" she screams. "We're innocent!"

"So your husband did not mean to hack your landlord to death?"

For a minute she freezes, as if the blade were falling on her, through her. Then she thrusts her face at him; he feels her spittle. "We worked on that farm all our lives and they were going to throw us out like animals, because they wanted to build big houses, big gardens."

"You remember your father, Noland?"

She goes for his face, her fingers stretched like claws.

105

The sun is high and the field is white. It's close to noon. A man is pacing around the hut, his wife pleading with him. Earlier he was in the field, fixing a water pipe; a paddy fish was caught in it. The landlord's foreman came, a surprise visit—he usually comes only during the harvest. He was friendly, even got down on his knees to help him rescue the fish. They had a laugh, then a smoke. Then slowly the news about the planned subdivision, because the landlord must diversify. The voice was apologetic, saying nothing will happen until after the next harvest and his family can stay for as long as he likes even after that, until the construction begins, of course.

The rescued fish stopped struggling in his grip. His fingers burrowed into the gills; a bone stuck into his palm. The sun disappeared in the sky, even as it burned his face.

"No, you're not going there, not like this," says his wife, but even his ears have died. Only his skin feels real, stinging in every pore as he walks out, walks to the big house, just as the landlord is getting into his Mercedes for a lunch in town without his usual bodyguards.

His ears have died like his eyes, all silent and dark, but his arms, his chest, all his flesh feels the warm spurt as he hacks and hacks. This is for my son, my father, my father's father—all of us that you've erased from this land.

106

From the door of the hut, the boy is watching. In the bedroom his mother prays, rocking herself before the pictures of her ancestors. The boy spots the little hill on a hill. He keeps watching, even when the sun hurts his eyes.

Uniforms suddenly block his view, asking questions, but the words are stuck in his throat and he keeps watching through the space between their shoulders, so they barge in. The butt of a rifle grazes his head. His mother drags him from the door, squeezing the breath out of him. The uniforms shout their questions, their voices high and frenzied. One slaps her; she begins to cry. He doesn't want her to cry so he points to the little hill on the hill, finding it hard to speak. One of the men pats him on the head, makes a phone call and sends the others away. His mother slaps him and cries, "What have you done?" and he wonders if the men asked her to slap him too. Together they stare at the hill. Nothing. The uniforms take her into the bedroom.

The boy covers his ears. His mother is crying louder, pleading, no, please, no, crying for his dead grandmother and the men cry out too, as if they're in this big, loud prayer together, then the crashing and thumping and she's shrieking, "My legs, my legs," the pitch so sharp it cuts through his chest. Then silence. He squints. Is that a stick figure on the hill? It's racing up, furiously. He keeps squinting. He's afraid it's climbing too early for the winged ones.

107

They fly low, or used to, and they're not angels. "The doves who fly low." This euphemism of decent folk, like "ladies of the evening," is outdated. It has long flown away with the girlie bars that used to thrive in this part of the city.

Again he tries the door of the moneychanger's. It's

locked. Did he not turn his cap around for luck? He sighs, he misses the girls. They fed him, sometimes gave him a bed. He'd look up their short skirts and they'd spank him, fuss over him and call him "cute." Things got better with Bobby, but he missed them, the softness of their skin when they crept into bed in the early morning. Now he can't trust the few who hide behind a shop like this, respectably beckoning foreign cash. They call him "bad luck," complaining he'll bring the police on them too. He abandons the door. He was hoping to plead with the owner, Auntie Carmen, to let him use the shower. She'd have cursed him, chased him away. Don't fly in my neighborhood.

How low can anyone fly? The skyline cuts, the gravel bruises — as sharp and hard as "decent folk."

Under a flashing Coke ad, the boy waits for a jeepney. He'll go back to the intersection. They can't turn him away on Christmas Eve.

Close by, two men watch him from a car. One makes a phone call and nods to the other, then they quickly move in.

108

He's afraid there's no angel waiting up there because there's no star yet, of course. The stick figure is halfway up. Sometimes it disappears, swallowed by the brightness. He squints to bring it back. In the bedroom, the big prayer has abated.

The uniforms walk out. They squint with him and make more phone calls, alerting a deployment ahead, closer to their quarry. Soon they trudge toward the hill, less anxious now, but not the boy. He feels hot and cold as the uniforms recede into the white light, growing more distant, unreal. He wants the brightness to swallow the stick figure on the hill again, or the dark to swallow the brightness, so the stars can come out, then the winged creatures. But first he must push the sun from its height. Make it sink. Trick the field from white to gold, quickly now. Then the dark will follow.

It's so silent inside the hut. He wants to call out to her, but his throat is a dry well. He tells himself she's praying silently.

He shifts uneasily; his pants are wet. He wants to shut his eyes so he can bring on the dark in his head, but he's too afraid to lose the first climber, more so now. Other stick figures are going up, but the very first one is already high up, so the boy takes heart. He claps his hands, wordlessly he cheers. It's like a big race and he feels as if he's running too, he's sweating, panting as the others gain ground, and he knows the angels won't come because the sun is high and it's hot and the field may never turn to gold.

He races, feet pounding on the pavement, vibrating his jaws or maybe it's just his screaming fuck you-fuck you at the men behind and whoever squealed at the pool joint, or at the world about to nab him. The swearing in English powers his legs, makes him invincible until the next corner, where the plainclothes police grab him. One starts the car, the other drags him to it but he slips away, swearing at the top of his lungs. He sprints again, ducks into alleys, he knows this territory—c'mon, try and get me, motherfuckers! But the men know more, the sickos on the prowl, the pimps on the prowl for sickos, the children prowling with pimps and sickos— the boy breaks into a halt, steps back. This can't be, the alley is closed off! He keeps stepping back, taking in the tall buildings on both sides, the men moving in, the fucking new wall behind him—he pulls out his gun, the men say, drop it, he shakes his head, I'll shoot, I'll kill you both, you pricks, he grows ten feet tall as a string of curses in English spills from his mouth, he grows as high as the wall, he pulls the trigger.

The heat cuts through his gut. He looks at it, bewildered, a little hole quickly blooming. He looks at the men, one of them still pointing a gun at him. His bewilderment grows. He's lost all his English; his mouth can't even form a swear word in his own tongue.

It falls, a stick figure rolling down the hill, and the boy sneaks down the wooden steps and keeps walking, tracing the familiar path. His father always goes there when he's worried. That little hill on the hill. He says close to the sky he can think. The boy tells himself his mother is still praying, so he goes alone. The rice embankments are dry so his feet don't sink, and the earth is burning so he sprints. This close the rice isn't really white. It's green and still. There's no wind. Once in a while there's a red or yellow flag signaling from afar, but it's only a canna lily. It makes the green greener—a trick of the eyes, his father tells him.

Don't let your eyes play tricks on you, son. Look first, then close your eyes, and draw it in your head. Make it yours in there. This blade of rice, the tree trunk, the brook behind the hut, that little hill on the hill. So you don't forget. But how could you, it's in your name. I gave it to you for remembering. *Noland. No land.* And why is that? Don't forget to keep asking, don't betray our hands. My father and my father's father farmed this land, and they never forgot. You see, the head looks small but it's big enough to carry a whole farm and all the hands that worked on it.

So he's walking up to look.

When the fields turn gold, the boy finds himself crouched in the bushes, shivering. Earlier, he stumbled over a body with red all over it. It looked familiar but not quite. The face was also covered in red and dirt; it felt sticky. The eyes were looking up, trying not to forget the sky.

When he comes out of hiding, he's still afraid but he must look again before night falls. He must not let his eyes play tricks on him. So he looks and looks. This is how a neighbor finds him. Squatting in the dark, silent at his father's feet.

111

Look closely. Around the city, men divine their palms and hold them up to their ears to listen, or speak. An intimation of fate, but from afar it looks more like a child's gesture, like leaning against the hand to sleep. Or perhaps a pensive, thinking act.

It is a circuit of divination with minuscule phones transmitting a singular fate: the other boy is dead, shot, accidentally.

Roberto looks at the boy squatting in the middle of the room, looking up at him. He sees the full story passing on his face. He turns off his phone and instinctively stretches a hand toward him. "It's okay now, Noland," he says. "You can go."

The boy keeps looking at him, his hand, as if the tale has ended there.

"It's okay," he says again and the boy opens his

mouth. He imagines he hears a sound, a word—he wants to hear it desperately. "What is it, child?"

"Noland?" the mother asks, dreading the usual whimper, but her son closes his mouth again, his arms.

"What were you going to say?" Roberto falls on his knees, both hands extended now.

"Don't you dare touch him!" the mother snaps, rescuing her son.

Roberto drops his hands, quickly rising. What's got into him? This interview is over. Only two will go to the safe house now. He opens the door to call for the car, but can't bring himself to leave. He wants to say something, do something, but he's afraid to look back.

He should know better. When a story is told, there's nothing much to do. The air does it for us, replenishes our lungs because we've lost so much in the telling, but even this air is thick with story. It feeds us back what we've just told, so it's difficult to breathe.

The mother clutches her son tighter, making it harder to breathe, but the boy cranes his neck to keep looking at the man who asked them so many questions. The mother wonders why he's silent, no sound of distress at all.

He is silent because he knows. He is sure now. That stick figure, that body on the hill. *His father.*

112

He remembers something else, before the neighbor finds him. He's waiting for the stars, the angels. His father is waiting too, eyes open. The boy goes up the little hill on the hill to search the sky better, to make certain that *they* will descend, then returns to the other waiting man. They wait a long time, wondering whatever happened to their wings.

The whole city waits. One more hour and it will be Christmas. The churches are set for the midnight mass. The choirboys are rehearsing hope and joy, so they can burst from their lungs in perfect harmony. The houses are breathless, the kitchens more so, the children pestering grown-ups—is it time yet? The fireworks are longing for their momentary lives. But not the stars or the trees. They've been flashing every night since September. Christmas is taken very seriously here.

Beside a canopy of light a woman turns in a drugged dream, waiting to finally wake. Under a giant star, a man waits for traffic to lead him home. Another man combs the streets for the boy he will lead home. The widow waits too on her bed, for what, she doesn't know. Only the senator knows of early good tidings divined on his palm after an auspicious beep. But not for the young reporter shocked at the story flashing on a little window: it's as if he died. At the intersection, lives are also waiting to cross with luck, while a mother and her son wait for the morning.

EPILOGUE

He is in a safe house. He does not know this house or this neighborhood. Nor how they got here. He does not know the men who took them here. He only knows what is in his head. He closes his eyes. He begins again.

Stars in the sky. The hill. And then?

It is harder to draw. There are no angels. He begins again. The deeply thinking face breaks and quickly mends his mother's heart. She is very sad, very proud. He does not whimper, he does not weep.

How to draw a Christmas fairy tale? It's time to help. We begin right here. We look closely at the boy and the mother. We draw wings on him, on her, we let them fly through the locked window, to the canopy of fairy lights, to a woman on a hospital bed. We make sure she too sprouts wings, make sure they fly together, glide over bodies in a morgue to finally find the other boy who needs his own pair. We make him test them, make him join the flight back to that hill where the man with open eyes sees four winged creatures descending—we hesitate, but we take our chance and draw his own pair, flawed but taking off with them back to the sky, all five points of light.

ACKNOWLEDGMENTS

Thank you to Carlomar Daoana, Annette Soriano-Ward, Nilo Candelaria, Medge Samblaceño-Olivares, Ma. Trinidad Maneja, Benhur Arcayan, Luis Liwanag, and all the "angels" who led me to the stories. To David Blackall, Margaret Gee, Susan Hawthorne, Reinis Kalnins, Connie Jan Maraan, and Elizabeth Pomada, and to Anna Rogers who helped me see and hear the stories clearly. To Caitlin Alexander and Kay Scarlett, who have kept believing in them. To PP, who has nourished both stories and storyteller. To all those who, with a passion, have guarded the human right of children to be children.

Merlinda Bobis was born in Albay, Philippines. The author of poetry, fiction, and drama, she has received the Prix Italia, the Steele Rudd Award for the Best Published Collection of Australian Short Stories, the Philippine National Book Award, the Judges Choice Award (Bumbershoot Bookfair, Seattle), the Australian Writers' Guild Award, the Carlos Palanca Memorial Award for Literature, and most recently the Philippine Balagtas Award, a lifetime achievement award. Her first novel, *Banana Heart Summer,* was short-listed for the Australian Literature Society Gold Medal. She lives in New South Wales, Australia.

DON'T MISS